# Self-Portrait
# with Wings

# Self-Portrait with Wings

## SUSAN GREEN

LITTLE, BROWN AND COMPANY
Boston   Toronto   London

First Edition

The characters and events in this book are fictitious. Any similarity to
real persons, living or dead, is coincidental and not intended by the
author.

Library of Congress Cataloging-in-Publication Data

Green, Susan Kohn.
Self-portrait with wings : a novel / by Susan Green. — 1st ed.
    p.   cm.
    Summary: Ten-year-old Jennifer's overnight acquisition of gossamer
wings brings her a combination of joy, drudgery, and embarrassment,
and she finds that the ice skating rink is the one place where she can
truly enjoy her new ability to fly.
    ISBN 0-316-32677-1
    [1. Flight — Fiction. 2. Ice Skating — Fiction.]   I. Title.
PZ7.R82633Se   1989 [Fic] — dc19   88–25000-CIP   AC

10  9  8  7  6  5  4  3  2  1

HC

Published simultaneously in Canada
by Little, Brown & Company (Canada) Limited

Printed in the United States of America

FOR ELIZABETH,
who wrote a wonderful fourth-grade
short story about a little girl who
sprouted wings.
Thanks, sweetheart.

I *WOULD LIKE TO THANK*
Maria Modugno of Little, Brown, my
agent, Jean Naggar, Carol Stacks, for her
continuing support, my dear, dear family,
of course, and Car Seip, Bob LaCrosse, and
the whole gang, especially Archie Walker,
at the Ice Studio. Archie, thanks for
the spin.

# Contents

1 · The Rink  3
2 · Home  12
3 · The Self-Portrait  18
4 · Wings  23
5 · On the Way to School  31
6 · Dawn  37
7 · On the Way Home  50
8 · Trying Dawn Out  62
9 · Wing Covers  70
10 · Responsibilities  79
11 · The Jennifer Jump  86
12 · Flying  95
13 · Disaster, Total Disaster!  107
14 · On the Way to the Dance  118
15 · The Dance  130
16 · I Don't Want Them Anymore  143

17 · Stuck — Again!  *151*
18 · The Accident  *160*
19 · Telling Her Mother  *168*
20 · They Go  *179*
21 · Freestyle  *190*
22 · Happiness  *204*

# Self-Portrait with Wings

# The Rink

"It is not," Jennifer said aloud, "fair."

Penelope was skimming over the ice, her arms perfectly rounded and balanced, the rhythm of her legs dipping step by step as her crossovers picked up speed. Then she poised, ready for her mohawk combination.

The others in her class watched as the mohawk took her into a backward spiral, more back crossovers, and then the three turn onto her outside edge. The ending was perfect, posed, the way the skaters did it in the Ice Capades. She even looked like a star in her pink tights and skating dress.

"Wonderful," said Scott. "Now, Jennifer."

Jennifer was wearing old blue jeans and a faded crimson sweatshirt that said San Francisco on it.

She grinned, then made her "sick duck face" as she took her position. Arms out, a little stiff, they did not have that graceful arch. And her legs never seemed to have the smooth action that Penelope's did. Jennifer's mother said that Penelope's center of gravity was lower. Jennifer had long, skinny arms and legs and was high-waisted. Her center was high. And her arms jerked when she took those long strokes. Penelope's arms were rounded, and they sort of swooped along with her body.

Jennifer poised for the mohawk. Her right foot was down now, opening the space as she turned to skate backward. She felt herself free, almost whizzing across the ice. Then the three turn, and again that feeling of flying as the ice swept under her. She caught sight of herself in the mirror. How could she feel as if she were flying and still look like a stick? She posed at the end, trying to look like the skaters in the Ice Capades, too.

Her toe pick caught the ice and she wobbled.

"Much better," said Scott carefully, "but a little more on that outside edge when you turn. Jennifer, are you listening? You can't concentrate when you're watching yourself, monkey. Now, remember" — he was demonstrating as he spoke — "when you turn, turn your shoulders as far as possible. Your feet won't have a choice. They have to follow. And . . . now . . . turn." He stepped back. "Now, let's see you do it again. And bend those knees!"

Jennifer got back into position and went through the routine. Somehow it didn't feel the way Scott looked.

"Better," he nodded when she was through. "A little more on that outside edge and you'll have it."

One day, she thought to herself as she skated back to the end of the line, one day he'll say "Wonderful!" to me, too. She could just see herself sailing into a split jump high above the ice. She leaned back against the barre and looked around The Rink.

It was tiny, like a doll's house. And Jennifer loved

it. She loved the whole idea that it was hidden away on the second floor of a brownstone on Madison Avenue in New York, over a French bakery. No one would even know it was there unless he or she were looking for it, or saw the kids going in with their skates swinging over their shoulders. The door was even set back from the street, sandwiched between French Pastry on one side and the dangling wrought-iron sign that said Attic Antiques on the other.

The door led to a narrow flight of stairs that climbed steeply to a landing. And there, another heavy, dark door opened to the rink, with the worn, cozy lounge, like a little log cabin, on one side, and on the other a long wall of Plexiglas windows overlooking the white world of light. Outside the tall windows, the trees were just beginning to bud. But inside was a cold, silvery postage stamp–sized rink, frosty and sparkling, with a long wall of mirrors echoing the white walls and smooth ice.

"Jennifer, are you watching? Or am I doing this for myself?" Scott's voice cut into her vision. "When you come out of the waltz jump, I want to see the stretch. Now, Angela."

Angela grinned and shrugged as she skated out from the group at the barre. She looked at Jennifer and winked. She was just there because they were best friends and had started skating together in kindergarten. And if she didn't take skating, her mother would make her take something else; something she'd have to practice — like piano.

She went through the steps like a rag doll, as usual, her arms sort of flopping around her. At the end she didn't bother to pose, but spurted to the barre and leaned back.

Scott watched and sighed deeply. "OK, Angela. Well, you managed to do the steps, but please, this time put some oomph in it. You look like an exhausted goldfish." Angela had red hair and was wearing her gold sweatsuit. She slumped against the barre, her arms wrapped over the railing as if it were holding her up. Scott glared at the class as he heard a giggle or two. "How are you going to manage a minute-and-a-half program if you can't get some energy going?"

"Don't worry, I'll be fine."

"Do it again."

"Do I have to?"

"Again, monster."

Angela giggled. This time, Jennifer thought, she looked like an overwound tin mouse as she raced through it.

"Da-daa!" she sang triumphantly at the finish, her arms outstretched wide.

Scott stood there shaking his head. "That," he said sorrowfully, "was pitiful."

She grinned at him. "Well, you said you wanted some energy. Want me to do it again?"

"I'd be afraid of what I'd get. But, Angela, when you do that waltz jump . . ."

Overhead the lights flickered on and off. "Saved by the bell." He ruffled Angela's hair as he passed her. "Just try to look as if you care next time. OK, monkey?"

The lesson was over. Now it was time to play.

At least it used to be time to play. Now everyone was getting ready for her first big freestyle test and it was mostly practice time. It was too bad, Jennifer thought, that everyone was getting so serious about everything. They used to kid around and giggle a lot. Now they just practiced and had contests: who could get lowest on a lunge or could walk fastest backward on her toe picks or jump the highest or do the most turns in a spin. She almost always lost. Stacey and Miranda were older and had longer legs. They were always fastest at everything. And Penelope was so good that she just went off by herself.

"Are you taking any private lessons before the test?" Angela asked as they hung on to the barre watching Miranda and Stacey skating backward.

"I dunno. Are you?"

"I guess so." She sighed. "My mother says that we can't spend all this money unless I can prove I'm serious about it. Serious! Me! She's even talking ballet. It's getting to be more like school than fun."

They looked up as Penelope glided by in her spiral. "Mom wants me to look like that."

Penelope's leg was straight in a high arabesque, her back arched. And her head was up, leading her body around the ice in a perfect arc. When Jennifer tried a spiral she looked more like a pump handle. Her back stayed straight all the way from her neck down to her rear. Then her leg sort of flopped out behind like a hockey stick. At night, in bed, when she daydreamed about her freestyle, it was not like this at all. It was not even like Penelope's. It was flying, with triple toe loops and glorious spins that went on forever and were so fast she was just a blur. She could even hear the gasps of wonder that broke from a crowd of classmates who never dreamed that she was so good.

Fifteen minutes later the lights flickered and the girls headed for the door. They streamed out into the lounge, pulling at their gloves as they clattered down the steps and waded through the pack of snow-suited five-year-olds waiting for Kiddie Time. They threaded their way across the floor, heading for the worn wooden benches by the window, sidestepping the book bags, picking their way over the purple and pink scarves and around red and lavender jackets, jogging shoes, and boots. There were books and purses and broken strings of bracelets that had been dropped then stepped on with ice-skate blades. There were stains of hot chocolate splattered and splashed in dark pools, wiped up but never erased from the rubber tiles.

The girls flung themselves on the benches next to a rack of skating costumes, shoved the coats aside, and leaned back. They pulled off their skates and sat staring at their feet while they wiggled their toes.

"I'm not sure they're all there. Can you feel yours?"

". . . my edges were wobbly, but he said they were better."

"Mom says I can have a sleepover after the dance," Stacey said. "Are you going, Jen?"

"It's gonna be so fun!" Angela giggled. "Remember last time? We put the gooey worms in Heather's sleeping bag?"

"I meant to the dance."

"When did you put on that nail polish?" Miranda squealed as Angela pulled off her thin skating sock and stretched out her legs.

"Oh, Mom won't let me out with it on my fingers, so this is the next best thing. Look pretty good, don't they? Spotlight Pink." Angela leaned back to admire them and wiggled her toes again. Then she put on her lilac sock with the black and pink snowflakes. "What are you doing this weekend?" she asked.

Jennifer stared at a sliver of ice sliding down the blade of her skate, then bent over to undo her laces. "I'm not sure." Her voice was muffled as she tugged at her skate. "I think Mom has to work, so I guess I'll just hang around and do stuff." Actually Jennifer liked staying home. She was so busy most of the time that it was a treat to have nothing to do. "What about you?"

"I guess we're going to our country shack." Angela grinned again. "Dad says that this year we're going to start getting it ready early, so when summer comes he can relax. Fat chance!"

"My mother signed me up for extra lessons," Penelope volunteered.

"Of course she has," Angela whispered at Jennifer. "Her mother even chose her music for her freestyle."

Penelope was sitting alone on the bench across from them, carefully drying her blades with a crimson towel. She was the only one who brought her own towel to clean her skate blades. She was the only one who always wore a skating dress or had leg warmers and mittens to match. She even had boot covers for her skates to keep them clean. Most of the time her mother came to watch the lesson or brought her for practice. "We're not even going away for spring vacation," Penelope said. "My mother says I have to practice for my freestyle."

"Oh, you're always practicing." Angela sounded bored.

"We never go away, anyway, so it doesn't matter to me," said Jennifer. "I guess I should come practice, too."

"Oh . . . maybe I'll see you." Jennifer looked up quickly. Penelope sounded funny, even a little shy. "Maybe we could get together or something."

"Maybe." Jennifer was noncommittal. Penelope always seemed so different from the rest of them; Jennifer didn't know what they'd do together or talk about if it wasn't skating.

Angela stretched, then fumbled under her seat for her PBS bag. She searched blindly on the bottom for change, then headed for the hot chocolate machine, as usual. "Want some?"

"Mmmmmmm."

They fed their quarters into the machine, then pressed the button. "What about you, Penelope?" Angela asked needlessly. "Aren't you having any?"

The girl looked at them wistfully from across the room and shook her head. Her mother always took her downstairs to the French bakery after skating. Jennifer's mother never did. She said it was a waste to spend three dollars and fifty cents on a piece of cake and another two dollars for something to drink. Jennifer thought it would be wonderful.

"Penelope?" Her mother had appeared in the doorway.

"Well, I have to go." Penelope stood, uncertain. "Jennifer, do you think —"

"Honey," her mother's soft voice interrupted her, "we're going to be late if you don't hurry. You have a piano lesson, remember?"

"Jen, look, they've got a new dress!" Angela was pulling a red and black costume off the rack and was holding it up to herself. "Isn't it gorgeous?"

Jennifer turned to the dresses. "I like this one." She had been dreaming about the white lace dress for months, ever since she had first seen it. It made her think of the snow princess from *The Nutcracker.* And now that she was going to do her first freestyle test, maybe her mother would buy it for her. They were waiting to see if it would go on sale.

"Let's go."

They clambered down the steps, their skates slung over their shoulders, their bags swinging heavily against their legs. As they passed the bakery they could see Penelope sitting at a small table with her mother. She was sipping hot chocolate that was topped with a cloud of whipped cream. Her mother was in her mink coat again. She always looked just perfectly beautiful. When Jennifer's mother came to pick her up she was usually in her corduroys and the down coat she had named "Old Purple." Penelope looked up and waved.

They stopped next door, as usual, and stared up at the dress in the bridal shop window. Today it was a creamy satin with a low-waisted sash that ended in a huge bow. In the middle was a diamond clip.

"Isn't it beautiful," breathed Angela. "That's the dress I want when I get married."

"You say that every time. Let's go."

At the corner the girls waited until the bus came; Angela hopped on, searching for her bus pass in the depths of her bag. When the door closed Jennifer turned and headed for home.

# 2

# *Home*

Jennifer lived on the twentieth floor of an apartment building near the East River. Two people and a poodle got into the elevator with her, so she waited until she had reached her floor before she started to whistle. It was her signal. By the time she reached her door she could hear Cleopatra scratching on the other side. As soon as it opened, the dog was all over her, wiggling and bowing with joy. She patted Cleo on the head and let her skates drop off her shoulders.

"OK, OK! Down, Cleo . . . down, girl. Hi, Mom!"

"Hi." Her mother's voice sang in from the other room. "I'm working."

That meant that her mother was in the bedroom where she had her studio. Jennifer went into the kitchen and poured herself a glass of milk. Cleo looked up at her expectantly, her head tilted to one side, her ears up, as if she were asking a question. "No," said Jennifer. "You can't have any. You're getting too fat."

The dog wagged her tail.

"Don't beg. It's not dignified." Jennifer reached

down to pet her, then reached for the Oreos. The dog's tail thumped against the floor.

"NO!" Jennifer took a couple of Oreos and wandered into her mother's room, munching. Cleo padded after her, still hopeful, her long, golden tail swishing back and forth.

The room was a mess. And her mother was still in the jogging suit she'd worn when she'd walked the dog that morning. That meant things were going well. When things were neat Jennifer knew that her mother was not really into her work.

"Hi, Mom."

Her mother looked up. There was a streak of crimson across her nose. "Hi, sweetheart. How was the skating?"

"OK."

"That's all?"

"Well, Penelope was great, as usual."

"Oh?" Her mother sounded as if she knew what was coming.

"I was awful. I just stink."

"Really? Come 'ere . . . hmmmmm." She sniffed at her daughter. "You smell perfectly good to me."

"You know what I mean."

"I'm afraid I do. I bet you were just fine."

"I was not. I look like a pump handle."

"Honestly, Jen, what are you talking about?"

"I wish I could be like . . ."

She heard her mother sigh. She knew just what her mother was going to say. "Honey, you're not heading for the Olympics. First of all, you're not even twelve yet, and this is supposed to be fun, remember?"

"Mmmmmm, I guess."

"And Penelope works very hard at it. Now, if you

want ballet lessons three times a week and skating five times a week, we can talk about it. Of course, we might not be able to eat for three or four days a week, but . . ."

Jennifer made her sick duck face and crossed her eyes.

"And thirdly . . ."

"I know, I know, her center of gravity is lower."

Her mother grinned. "Have you heard all this somewhere before?"

"Mmmmmm."

"Anyway, I bet your spins are coming."

"Yeh . . ." Jennifer had to admit that her spins were one of her strong points. "I guess so."

"Now, let me finish up here and you can get to your homework. Do you have much?"

"Medium. There's a math quiz, and I have to draw a picture of our house."

"Oh, that's fun. Inside or out?"

"In. And Stacey wants me to come over before the dance . . . we're having a sleepover. And I need a new skirt for it."

"We can talk about it over dinner, sweetheart. Sweet and sour chicken tonight." It was Jennifer's favorite. "And your father called. He wants to know how your Hebrew test went." Jennifer's parents were divorced and her father lived in Florida. He called every once in a while, but long distance was so expensive. She wished he lived closer. "He has something to tell you."

"What?"

"I don't know. He wanted to know when your freestyle is."

"Oh." Jennifer's heart gave a little flip-flop.

"And put your glass in the sink when you're finished with it," her mother called after her as she went out. "And put your skates away!"

How did she always know when her skates weren't away?

"And hang up your jacket!" Jennifer scooped the jacket off the hall chair and went toward her room. She'd have to decide what to draw for school.

Jennifer loved their apartment. She loved it because it was small and cozy. And she loved her bedroom. Once it had been part of the living room, but someone had built a wall and made this tiny nook of a room. Her mother had wanted to decorate it but Jennifer had said no. She didn't want anything that matched. It would look as if it came out of a magazine instead of a place that was really hers. So there was her bed with the flowered comforter that was getting old and flat and the sheets that almost went with it, but really didn't. And the bookcases with her stuffed animals and old dolls and games and books and the things she had made at camp. Maybe she'd draw that.

She threw her jacket on the window seat. It was her favorite place in the whole world. There were drawers under it where they kept some of her clothes, and butterfly cushions on top. From there she could look out over the whole city. Sometimes she thought it was just like Heidi's loft. At night she watched the stars and the city lights sparkling.

In the winter she watched the snowflakes play with the glow around the street lamps down below. They seemed to circle lazily, then dash against it, then fall upward toward her. When she had had the flu she had flown her kite out the window and up into the sky above the city. She had felt it tugging at her hand as if it were alive, as if she had held a bird on the end of a string — a bird that wanted to fly.

Now she sat down and gazed out. There were a couple of sea gulls overhead. They swooped, their wings outstretched. They simply lay on the invisible air and were carried from side to side, gently soaring, so freed from the sidewalks where she had to walk that Jennifer felt carried away with them when she watched them from her window. Sometimes that was how she felt when she was skating.

She shifted her weight on the window seat and absentmindedly petted Cleopatra's head. "What do you think Daddy wants to know about freestyle for?" she asked. He had never even seen her skate. If he wanted to know when her freestyle was, maybe . . . Her heart gave a little jerk inside her.

"Jennifer," her mother's voice interrupted her, "are you missing anything?"

She was standing in the doorway holding her backpack. "It weighs a ton," she said. "From the feel of this thing you have a load of work, sweets." She let it drop with a thud. "You'd better get started or you'll be up all night.

"Oh, and I have something for you. I almost forgot." In her hand was a box of colored pencils. "They're gorgeous. Some of them are even iridescent. When you're finished with your homework you can try them out. And don't forget to call your father."

Sometimes Jennifer thought she would want to be an artist when she grew up. Her mother was pushing solar energy science.

Jennifer headed for the phone.

"Jen? I'm on my way out, so I can't talk long, but when did you say the freestyle was?"

"June twelfth, Daddy. Daddy? I got a B on the Hebrew, and . . ."

"That's great. Listen, I'm going to try to make it to see you skate. I think I can get away for a day or so. OK?"

"Really!"

They had talked for a few more minutes, then he had had to leave. Now she stared out the window. "My dad's coming," she said to the gulls. "He said he was going to try." She could just see the surprise on his face when he saw her spins. She got up and did a pirouette on the rug.

"Jen, are you working?" Her mother's voice came floating in.

She zipped open her backpack, took out her books, and got to work.

# 3

# The Self-Portrait

Jennifer was drawing wings.

At one time she had drawn rainbows — millions and millions of rainbows. Then she had drawn rainbows over flowers, then rainbows and clouds. Lately she had been drawing people and, since they had moved to the twentieth floor, birds. Now she was working on "Self-Portrait with Wings."

It was far more complicated than she had imagined.

First of all, contrary to what she had originally thought, wings just couldn't stick out of her back. At the Natural History Museum there was a whole case showing how a bird was put together. The wing bone was sort of set into the shoulder blades just the way her arms were, then attached to the sides of the body and across the back. As she had stood in front of the case she had suddenly realized that all those angels' wings she had always seen were ridiculous. If an angel did have wings, she'd have to have two sets of shoulder blades and two sets of muscles to go along with them. And the arms and the wings would have to be attached at the same place. But then they'd get in the way of each other all the time. And besides, she'd be back-heavy. She'd be falling over backward all the time. Jennifer was sort of disgusted with the old masters. They really hadn't thought out the problem very well. Their angels were not anatomically correct. Her mother said it didn't matter. What they did was beautiful and they had what she called "artistic license," anyway. That meant they could do anything they wanted to as long as it looked good. But Jennifer thought they were cheating.

And there was something else the old masters hadn't thought of. Any wing that would be big enough to hold up a human being would have to be huge. Birds had hollow bones to make them light. Jennifer didn't. The old masters didn't know what they were doing, she thought. Maybe one of her mother's anatomy books would help.

Her mother had hundreds of books, all smushed together in the bookcase, and loads and loads of them were anatomy books: animal anatomy, human anatomy, *The Artistic Anatomy of Trees*. Jennifer hadn't even known that trees had anatomy.

She passed her fingers over the books so she wouldn't miss what she was looking for. In between *Miss Manners' Guide to Rearing Perfect Children* and *My Friends the Wild Chimpanzees* was *A Handbook of Anatomy for Art Students*. That was it.

It was a thick book. The pages were very worn, thumbed over and over again, the text underlined in yellow marker. Jennifer rolled her thumb over the pages. "Back . . . back . . . shoulder . . . shoulder," she murmured. On page fourteen she came to a picture of the back of a skeleton. She studied the figure carefully. That was the one. But she couldn't find any place to add a wing. Again and again she fitted sheets of tracing paper over the picture and traced the back. She tried fitting a wing over the shoulder blade. That didn't work. It would be whacking into the arm all the time.

She put it under the arm. That was ridiculous. She even drew it coming out of the arm. She put it on top and underneath and the pile of crumpled papers grew. There was no way it could work. People were not meant to have wings.

She crushed up one more drawing and hurled it at the pile on the floor. Cleopatra bounded after it and pounced. She brought it back to Jennifer and waited, wagging expectantly. When nothing happened she dropped the soggy paper on the window seat and put her head down on the cushion, eyeing the last Oreo on the plate. Jennifer put her hand on the dog's head and stared at the cushion next to her. The butterflies and dragonflies on the seat had different kinds of wings. They were huge! At least three times bigger than the bodies, but light and airy. And they came out from the center of the insects' backs. Obviously there was something about weight and balance there — and they even had arms! If dragonflies had arms, she thought, they'd be separate from the wings.

She felt her heart beating suddenly. It was right. She could feel it.

In the bookcase she found *Borne on the Wind* by Stephen Dalton. Then, on a new piece of tracing paper, she drew the skeleton one more time. Down the sides of the shoulder blades she drew a set of dragonfly wings, thin, wirelike lines strung together like a web. She pictured them on her back and wiggled her shoulders. The lighter the wing, the less her shoulder would have to move. A wiggle would do it.

Then she opened her sketchbook. Very carefully, looking in the mirror, she drew a self-portrait and added the wings. They looked just right; as if they belonged there. Finally she reached for her new set of glimmering, colored pencils.

A half hour later she was finished. The wings had looked OK before, but now they were wonderful! They looked real and just as if they really belonged to her. They glimmered and glistened like a moth's wings caught in the light, opalescent and transparent.

"Jen," her mother's voice floated in from the kitchen, "have you finished your homework?"

"Sure thing, Mom."

"Well, sweetheart, it's time for bed." She appeared in the doorway, wiping her hands on a towel, leaned over Jennifer, and looked at the drawing.

"Oh, Jen, that's wonderful!"

"Thanks, Mom."

"You're getting so good." She gave her a hug. "Now, finish up for tonight and clean up all of . . . that." She pointed to the pile of wrinkled papers on the floor. "And get ready for bed."

Her voice continued as she went back to the kitchen. "And put my books back, please.

"And," the voice came sailing in, "don't forget to pack your backpack for tomorrow."

Jennifer put the pencils away and they seemed to glimmer, even in the darkness of her desk drawer. Then she propped the picture up against the lamp by her bed, where she could see it as she drifted off to sleep. The wings were gossamer, shimmering with color. Unlike any colors she had ever seen, they seemed to move and glow on the page. She shifted and tried to think about her skating program. She saw herself gliding, like Penelope, over the ice, then leaping into a triple axel and floating smoothly to a stop.

Wouldn't it be lovely, she thought as she drifted off, wouldn't it be lovely to have wings.

# Wings

Jennifer was riding on the back of a bird. And there was music. It streamed across the sky like a ribbon and the bird followed it over the city — over the rooftops and into narrow city gardens tucked away. They followed it to a window, and when the bird stepped lightly through the pane of glass, its flat wings suddenly fanned out under her, turning to ice.

Jennifer glided on it.

At the other end of the rink people were singing. Their voices flowed into the ice and flared up around her, taking her spinning. When they released her, she sailed across the ice in a perfect arabesque as a golden medal floated toward her. It slipped over her head as the music turned to cheers. She turned to bow to a circle of light, hit a bump, and swayed.

Jennifer turned over and opened her eyes. A hint of gray light was seeping in through the slats of the venetian blinds. She snuggled down deeper into her flowered comforter and closed her eyes again.

"Go get Jennifer." Her mother's voice was faint in the other room. "Go on, Cleo, get Jennifer."

The dog came padding eagerly into her room. Jennifer reached out sleepily and draped her arm over Cleopatra's neck.

"Jen, it's time to get up." Her mother appeared in the doorway with a glass of orange juice in her hand.

"Noooooo."

"Not 'noooooo.' Now!"

"Mmmmmmm . . . I'm in the middle of a dream. Wait a minute."

"Up you go. Here's your juice." She put it down by the bed. "Vacation starts tomorrow. Then you can sleep as late as you want." She gave her a quick kiss, then headed back to the kitchen. Jennifer could hear her opening a can of dog food. She cuddled down deeper.

"NOW, JEN!"

A few moments later Jennifer was rolling out of bed. She reached for her clothes and started to dress. She had been dreaming about skating and her freestyle program. A spiral took her toward the dresser. In her underwear she tried a spin. It didn't work very well on the rug. She skated backward to the closet and reached up for a shirt, then slipped it on. Her arm fit easily through the sleeve, but when she put it over her back it sort of lumped up behind. She felt a strange catching, the same strange catching feeling, she thought, that she had had when she had turned over in bed. She had thought she was still asleep.

She took off her shirt and looked at it. It was the same as usual. Mom had even ironed it. Again she slipped it on and again it caught on something and seemed to float over her. What on earth was going on? She looked in the mirror. The shirt was floating high over her head, like an old-fashioned picture in a ghost story.

Jennifer turned around. There was nothing there. She faced the mirror. The shirt was still there, one arm in the sleeve, the rest of it looming somewhere in the air above her. She took it off and stared.

They hovered over her, nearly transparent and net-ted, like butterfly wings . . . No! . . . like dragonfly wings!

She turned to look behind her. There was no one . . . nothing . . . there. Only her room, looking as it always did. She spun around and in the mirror there they were again.

Wings! There were wings growing out of her back! Just like the . . . She stopped, then leaped to her bed. On the table, leaning against the lamp, was the picture she had drawn the night before. And the wings were gone! Those beautiful gossamer wings that had arched over her self-portrait were gone!

Still staring at the picture, she put her arm up behind her and felt her way up her spine. There was something there. Slowly she turned back to the mirror. They were looming above her, beautiful and transparent and real.

Real?

"Jennifer," called her mother's voice from the other room. "Are you getting dressed?"

"Yyy . . . yes, Mom!"

"Well, hurry up. You have to have something to eat before you leave."

That was normal. She'd never dream her mother was nagging at her to hurry. That was the way things really were. She sat down on the edge of her bed, her shirt hanging limply from her hand. Cleopatra was staring up at her. She growled low in her throat.

"Do you see them?"

Cleo tilted her head to one side, put her ears up, and looked past her, over her head. Again she made a sound deep in her throat.

"It's only me, Cleo." The dog was silent. "What am I supposed to do now?" Cleo stared at her.

"Jenny, are you coming? What are you doing in there?"

Jennifer sighed. "Let's go," she said and slowly headed out to her mother. Cleopatra trotted along with her.

"Jennifer Rosen, what are you doing out here like that? You're supposed to be dressed."

"Mom, do you see anything different about me?"

"Well, you don't have a shirt on. You can't go to school like that."

"But, Mom, don't you see . . . anything else?" She looked at her mother closely.

"No, and you're going to get awfully cold like that, so get a move on. You can't miss your bus this morning. You have a math test."

"Are you sure you don't see anything strange about me?"

"That's a leading question, Jen." Her mother put down the dish she was holding and looked suddenly anxious. "Jen, are you getting the chicken pox?" They had been expecting it for years.

"No."

"Jennifer, what am I supposed to see?" She was beginning to sound exasperated. "This is not the time to play twenty questions."

"You don't see any" — Jennifer took a deep breath — "wings?"

"Wings? Jennifer."

"You don't see them?"

"Go! NOW!"

Back in her room Jennifer was in a quandary. The wings were still there. Wow. In a way she sort of liked the idea. Invisible wings. That was special. A little tingle went through her. What a great secret! The only immediate problem was clothes. And what to do about school. She could say she was sick. But she hadn't been fast enough and her mom had one rule about being sick: If you weren't throwing up and didn't have a temperature, you went to school.

She headed for the bathroom, quietly closed the door, and sat down on the toilet seat. She had to think.

If she could convince her mother that she actually did have wings, then what would her mom do? She'd probably faint. But after that what?

She'd probably call the doctor. And he'd call in a specialist. And she'd probably end up as an article in a medical magazine. They'd probably want to amputate. She shivered at the idea of their cutting off her wings. Well, that was out.

Or, if she kept her wings she could end up in Ringling Brothers in an act like Tiny What's-His-Name and have to go on Johnny Carson and "Ripley's Believe It or Not." They'd probably make her do all kinds of tricks. People would think she was really weird. Maybe it was better that her mother hadn't noticed.

No, she couldn't tell her until she decided what she was going to do. For the time being she wasn't going to tell anyone.

"Jennifer Rosen, I am losing my patience! What are you doing now?"

"I'm in the bathroom!"

"Well, hurry up!"

Jennifer opened the door and peered out to see if her mother was in sight. She wasn't. She made a dash to her room, grabbed her shirt and sweater, dug into her drawer for a pencil and a pair of scissors, then sprinted back again. She closed the door as quietly as she could. Then she stood up to look into the mirror and decide where she should cut her clothes for the wing slits.

She slipped one arm into a sleeve and wiggled the shirt over her shoulders. With her other hand she made a pencil mark where she thought the cut should start.

Am I glad I drew dragonfly wings instead of butterfly, she thought. At least these'll be narrow enough to fit through my shirt. The little tingle of excitement rippled through her again at a new thought. I wonder if I can move them. She stood staring at herself in the mirror, transfixed by the idea.

She wiggled her shoulders and felt something. Cautiously she pressed her shoulders back and felt the wings slowly drop down behind her. She could fold them across her back. She could feel them against her legs. Slowly she pushed her shoulders forward and the wings rose a bit. They worked! Wow!

She twitched her shoulders and the wings twitched. She moved them slowly, then a little faster. She tried one shoulder at a time. In front of the mirror she twitched back and forth and her wings cooperated, folding and unfolding, dipping and twitching behind her. She could feel them stirring the air. She could see them moving and waving against the garden wallpaper behind her. She could almost see herself lifting off and floating around the rooms! out the windows! into the sky! She opened the wings wider. When they loomed up she looked like a huge Tinkerbell.

"JENNIFER!"

She grabbed her shirt and laid it down on the floor. She picked up the scissors, took a deep breath, and made the first cut.

She had never thought it would be so difficult to put on a shirt. She tried getting into it the conventional way, first one arm in and then over her back, but the wings were so long that the shirt didn't reach. She almost bent herself backward trying to hold the shirt out as far as possible with one hand while she tried to find the slits with the other. She twisted and turned, then bent in the other direction. She could feel the wings bending against the material as they got caught up in it, and once one got tangled going into a sleeve. As soon as she got that wing free the other one caught its tip under the collar. She could feel it bending further and further. It was going to snap! She panicked and let the whole thing go.

Panting, she stared at a hanger hung on the curtain rod. Maybe that would do it. She put it on the towel rack behind her, hung her shirt on it, turned around, and aimed.

It was not easy. When her wings caught the fabric the shirt swung. When one wing found a slit and went through, the other couldn't find its opening. Once, she got the wrong wing in the wrong cut and the whole thing swung around frantically, backward.

She spun around and glared at it. It slowed to a stop, hanging quietly.

They faced each other silently, then, very deliberately, she turned again, measured her distance, and thrust her wings simultaneously toward the shirt. Miraculously she felt her wings find the openings and slip through. No sudden movement, she thought, holding her breath as she slowly pulled her shirt up and over her shoulders. She twisted one arm back to find its sleeve, then the other. And praying that nothing would tear, she wiggled her way into it.

She sat down on the toilet seat, breathless, and felt her heartbeat slow as she buttoned up. At the thought of what she must have looked like, hopping around and jabbing at her shirt, she started to giggle. Until she saw her sweater. It was still lying at her feet. And she had to wear it. It was part of the school uniform. She kicked it and it skidded across the tiles to the bathtub.

"JEN!" There was a loud rap on the door. "What is going on in there? If you don't come out I'm coming in!"

Jen spun around, grabbed the sweater, and slashed at it quickly. She threw it over her shoulders. It would cover the cuts in the back of her blouse, anyway. She tied the arms in front of her. It was very preppie, but it was the best she could do.

She took one last look in the mirror. She looked almost normal, she thought in surprise. She slapped some water on her face and smoothed down her hair. Then she opened the door.

# 5

# On the Way to School

They always left the house together. Her mother said that it got her off to an early start and she liked having a leisurely walk together before the day really got started. Half the time, however, it was anything but leisurely. Her mother usually thought they were late, and Cleo zigzagged across the sidewalk, getting in people's way, trying to stop and sniff, while her mother pulled on the leash and tried encouragement. "Let's go. Come on, Cleo, let's run! Where's Jennifer, Cleo?"

Jennifer was either struggling with her backpack or stumbling on her laces that came untied or dreaming about her skating program.

Today, for the first time, Jennifer wished that her mother wouldn't like that leisurely time together.

She grabbed her backpack at the door and while Cleopatra squirmed with delight and her mother struggled to lock the door behind them, Jennifer hauled it out to the elevator.

In the elevator she was sure everyone would stare at her. But there was only an elderly man with very

thick glasses and Mrs. Sloan with her poodle, Muffin.
"Sit, Cleo." The dog sat and looked longingly up at
Muff. Jennifer's mother reached down and ruffled her
fur. "That's a good girl." Then all the heads tilted up
to watch the numbers light up as they descended.

Jennifer counted silently as one by one the numbers
lit. Fourteen, twelve. It was taking forever! Please
don't stop. Please don't let anyone else get on. Seven,
six, five . . . two . . . As the elevator opened Cleo
made a leap for the door, bombing through the lobby
toward the street, Jennifer's mother scrambling after
her on the other end of the leash. Jennifer fiddled with
her backpack straps to let everyone else off first. She
didn't want to take any chances. Then, lugging her
backpack behind her, she followed. She felt very
strange. She could feel the wings flopping against the
backs of her knees as she walked. It felt weird, like a
tail. On the street, Cleo reached her objective and
stopped short to sniff. Jennifer's mother reached up to
help her daughter. "Here, honey," she said, "let me
get that thing up onto your back." And she bent over
to pick it up. "Oh, my God," she groaned, "that weighs
a ton! What do you have in there?"

"Never mind, Mom, this is fine." Jennifer hadn't
thought of that. How could she wear a backpack with
wings?

"Do you really have to carry all of this back and
forth?" Her mother hoisted it off the ground.

"NO!" Jennifer heard her voice come out in a panicked screech. Her mother stared at her, the backpack
midair. "I mean, no, Mom, please. Nobody wears them
anymore. They'll just think I'm a jerk if I walk in with
that thing on my back."

Her mother looked at two girls passing by. "They're wearing them."

"They don't go to my school."

"I see," she said slowly, "so it's just in your school that no one wears backpacks anymore."

Jennifer thought fast. "We're starting a fad," she said.

"So you can be different."

"Right."

"Oh."

"Yap!" Cleo bounded suddenly, straining at the leash as she spied Corky at the corner. Jennifer sighed with relief as she yanked the backpack off the sidewalk and followed her mother, the bag banging against the front of her knees and a wing hitting the back of each leg with every step. Flip flop, flip flop, went the wings against her legs. The backpack was so heavy it was almost dragging on the street. Flip flop, flip flop.

"Jenny, what do you think?"

"Huh?" She was suddenly conscious that her mother was beside her again.

"You haven't heard a word I've said," she sighed. "I was talking about your vacation. I'm sorry we can't go away. But maybe we can do all those things we never get to do, like the Statue of Liberty and the World Trade . . ."

"I don't care. I think I just want to stay home, anyway."

"You do? I thought you wanted to go to the Virgin Islands, like Samantha did at Christmas."

Jennifer evaded her mother's eyes. "I need to practice a lot for my freestyle."

"Well, I'm glad. I thought you'd be . . . Oh, Cleo!"

The dog pulled her back. "You keep going, sweetheart. I don't want you to miss your bus."

Jennifer kept walking. Corky was bounding toward them, pulling his lady with him. She felt her wings; flip flop, flip flop. She started to walk faster; slap, slip, slap, slip. She pictured what her wings looked like as she walked along. The backpack was so heavy it was making her lopsided. She shifted it to the other arm, then wiggled her shoulders.

Suddenly she lifted.

It was only for a second. She really wasn't sure that it had happened.

"Ohmagod!" She looked around but no one was paying any attention. Her mother was untwisting the leashes where Corky and Cleo had gotten themselves tangled. And the two kids in front of her were talking. She'd better try to control her wings until she had some time to herself to experiment.

On the other side of the street she saw her bus coming. It was hard trying to run with the wings flopping around her knees and the backpack banging her shins.

"Whoops!" She lifted and skimmed the pavement again. This time the backpack dragged her over to one side and she landed, lopsided, stumbling. She straightened up and staggered on, waving wildly at the driver.

At the corner the light was changing. The traffic was edging up, ready to move, but she didn't want to wait. She charged across. Behind her she thought she heard her mother screech, but she tottered across the street, hoisted her backpack up onto the bus, and climbed up after it. Behind her the doors closed. "Someday you're gonna get killed pulling stunts like that," the driver muttered at her. "If you were my kid . . ." She pulled out her bus pass and headed for the back of the bus.

Seats on the bus were not made for wings. Jennifer scrunched herself down on an aisle seat and faced the windows, her wings hanging off the edge of the seat. *I don't believe it.* She slumped for a second, then giggled to herself. Maybe she wouldn't have to take the bus after this. Maybe she'd fly to school, get a little hang glider thing for her backpack, and . . .

"Hey, girlie, can I get in there or what?"

A burly man with a scowl on his face was looking down at her. She slid her legs around to let him in. And she felt him step on the tip of her wing as he pushed past.

"Ow!"

". . . hogging it all to herself," she heard him muttering. "These kids think they own the world." His voice drifted off as he turned his face to the window.

She shifted cautiously and put her hand behind her to feel her wing. It was still there. At least something was there, light and filmy with a starched feel to it.

Her eyes went past the man next to her to the people on the street. None of them looked as if they could have them either. They were all plodding along, their feet touching the ground.

Could she be the only person in the world with wings? She glanced up at the man in front of her. He was sitting up very straight against the back of his seat. And the woman on the street with the schnauzer; her feet didn't do anything surprising when the dog went after the bicycle. And if that jogger had them any little breeze would sweep her along; she wouldn't have to do all that legwork.

"Hey, girlie, ya gonna let me out or what?"

"Oh." She shifted to let the burly man by. He shoved her out of his way, then pushed his way to the door. She tried to picture him in the air and stifled a a giggle. No, definitely no wings.

But, if hers were invisible, maybe theirs were, too. From now on she'd have to look at people more closely. Maybe they were hiding wings, too. The thought made her shiver.

She almost missed her stop.

# 6

# Dawn

By the time she reached school she had a plan. The sidewalk was swarming with kids, but she ducked her head low, walked fast, and ploughed through as if she were in a hurry.

"Hey, Jen . . ."

"Gotta do math," she muttered and kept going. She ran through the great hall and headed for the stairs. If she could just get to her classroom, she'd be fine. She could feel the wings wobbling on her back as she scrambled up those last two flights, breathless, and staggered into her homeroom. No one was there.

Her seat was in the back. All she had to do was get her stuff out and sit. It was a short day. She just had to get through assembly; that was going to be the tricky part. She had to sing with chorus and that meant getting up on stage. Well, she'd figure that out later. What else? She opened her schedule book. Homeroom . . . great. Math; that was OK. She didn't have to go anywhere for that. She bent over her desk and began to get organized.

When the kids arrived she was ready. Her sweater was on, sort of lumped up in back, but no one would notice. Somehow she had managed to get it over her head and get the wings out the slits in the back. She sat with her head on her hands trying to look pale.

"Hey, Jen." Angela was busy pulling papers out of her bag. "Did you get the answer to number four? I can't understand this stuff." She unwrinkled the paper and smoothed it out on her desk. "What'sa matter with you? You look funny."

Samantha's singsong voice interrupted them. "Guess what, Ange, Judy sprained her ankle. Wanna try out for the team?"

"I don't know. Do you want to try out, Jen?"

"Jennifer?" Samantha clutched her heart and pretended to faint. "No, no, please, anything but that!" Jennifer looked at Angela and made her sick duck face. She was terrible at basketball *and* soccer *and* volleyball. She never made a team.

"I don't know," Jennifer said, "I don't think I can. I've gotta practice skating after school."

Samantha looked at Kathy and giggled. "Oh, yeah, skating. How about it, Ange?"

Angela shrugged. "Me, too . . . I forgot. We've got freestyle coming up."

"Too bad, you woulda been good. Hey, Heather, you wanna try out for the team?"

"Sure."

Jennifer felt hot. Why did Samantha always make her feel like such a jerk?

"Why does she do that?" Angela sounded annoyed. "She's such a pain. Not everybody has to play sports."

Jennifer shrugged. And felt her wings catch on the chair. She reached back and brushed them. They felt stiff. What if Samantha found out about them? Oh, God.

"Hey, guys." Peter came rushing in late, as usual, dropped his backpack, and threw himself in his chair with a clomp. "Did you hear about the Interschool Jog-a-Thon? You have people pay a nickel for every minute you jog and it goes to charity. All the schools are doing it."

"When?"

"I dunno. Over vacation sometime."

"Yuk. I've gotta go to the Bahamas." Tommy sounded disgusted.

Then Mr. Gomez came in and the day started. Jennifer breathed a sigh of relief.

It went pretty well, actually. They were all studying for the math test or talking about the dance or vacation and, for once, Jennifer tried to be quiet. There were a couple of rough spots: once when Heather said she was hot and the teacher asked David to open the window behind Jennifer. Jennifer could feel the wings ruffling suddenly on her back as a little breeze swooped in. She jumped in her seat, pressing her shoulders back, squirming to keep them from fluttering. Samantha looked over at her. "What's the matter, Jennifer, is something wrong?" David turned around and stared.

And again when Mr. Gomez asked Jennifer to collect the math papers: she stared at him blankly for a moment then stood up very carefully and edged her way down the aisle. She kept her back to the wall but everyone had been too busy shuffling papers to pay any attention to her. At the front of the room she almost threw the test papers onto his desk then edged back along the wall again. She just knew everyone was staring at her.

"Are you all right?" Angela was staring at her strangely as she got back to her desk. "You don't look so hot."

"I'm fine," she muttered, as she slipped into her seat. She sat very still, her heart beating fast, wings fluttering, and let out a long, trembling breath.

"OK, kids" — Mr. Gomez interrupted her concentration on the ruffling sensations that fluttered on her back — "don't forget, when swim is over you've got to change fast. You've got assembly and you can't be late. Now I know it's hard, but . . ."

Swim? Frantically Jennifer checked her schedule. She'd forgotten all about swim! And the instructors were tough; unless you were really sick you could never get out of swim. The bell rang and the kids scrambled to get out.

"Aren't you coming?" Angela was waiting for her, as usual.

Jennifer pretended to be hunting for something in her desk. Papers were shuffling all over the place and she dug down underneath them. One or two fell on the floor. She barely glanced up.

"Hey, guys." Stacey and Heather were standing at the door. "Are you coming? I wanna sign up for the Jog-a-Thon. The list is in the gym. Come on, Jen." Stacey sounded impatient.

"You guys go ahead," Jennifer mumbled at Angela. "I'll meet you. I've got to . . ."

Angela looked at her strangely again, then shrugged. "OK, Jen, but you'd better hurry." When she had disappeared through the door Jennifer sat back and looked at the ceiling. What was she going to do now? If she sat there, they'd come to get her, and if she went somewhere to hide, they'd be out looking for her. She couldn't go swimming, that was for sure.

Mr. Gomez's head stuck into the doorway. "Hey, aren't you supposed to be somewhere?"

She headed out into the halls. She could feel the sweater unraveling down the back; there must be something funny with one of the wings. A few kids passed her and she spun around, her back to the wall. They looked at her oddly, but went on. She had just reached back to tug at the wing, when she heard more faint voices. Oh, no! She scurried around the corner, ducked into a closet, and leaned back. She didn't know what to do. The muffled voices outside were closer. It sounded like Angela! Jennifer's heart beat wildly. She had to have help. If she just told Angela . . .

She opened the door a crack and listened again. The voices had faded. She peered out. Angela was alone in the corridor.

"Angela!" she hissed. There was no response. Angela kept walking. In a minute she would turn the corner.

Jennifer grabbed a broom standing by the door, then eased halfway out into the corridor. She pointed the handle toward her friend, lunged quickly, then leaped back to her closet.

"Ow!" There was a yelp from Angela. She spun around to see Jennifer wildly motioning to her. "What do you think you're doing! That hurt!"

"Shhhhh! Come here!" Jennifer gestured frantically, then disappeared into the closet.

Angela followed angrily, rubbing her side where the broom handle had struck. As soon as she was inside, the door was flung shut.

She whirled around to face Jennifer. "What's going on? You know, that hurt!"

"I had to . . . you were going to get away."

"Get away? What are you talking about?"

"Angela, I need you . . . you see . . ."

But Angela wasn't listening. "What are you doing in here? You're going to be late for swim. You know, you've been acting really weird, Jennifer."

"Angela, shut it!" She was almost screaming, if you could scream in a whisper. Angela stared at her. Jennifer looked frantic. Her hair was a mess, and there was something wrong with the way her sweater fit; it was lumpy or lopsided or something. "Angela, you've got to help me!"

"What is it? You look awful."

"Ange, please . . ."

Angela gave up and sighed. "OK, what is it?"

Now that Angela was within reach, Jennifer grabbed her arm and clutched at her.

"Are you my best friend?"

"Well . . . sure . . ."

"And best friends have secrets, right?" There was a defensive tone in Jennifer's voice that made Angela a little wary.

"What kind of secret?"

"It's a secret. I can't tell you . . . not until you say you won't tell."

"I don't know." Angela was beginning to be a little more than doubtful. "What's all the mystery?"

"You've got to promise first," said Jennifer stubbornly.

"Well, I don't know. Is this something my mother should know?"

"No, it's not that kind of secret. No one's grabbed

me and I'm not smoking or pregnant or anything."

For a moment Angela stood undecided. Jennifer was backed up funny, scrunched into a corner, up against some coats, as if she were afraid to move.

She gave up. "OK, I promise. But it had better be a good secret. I don't want to feel guilty or anything."

"Well." She was suddenly nervous. Now that Angela stood staring at her with a curious expression on her face, it was hard. "It's just that I've got this . . . problem."

There was a long silence.

"Yeah?"

"It just sort of . . . happened . . . to me."

"What?" Angela sounded impatient. "Look, Jen, we've got to get to swim, so either tell me or . . ."

"I . . . I . . ." Jennifer looked at her shoes. It was now or never. "I've got . . . wings," she whispered.

"Really? I've got a whole collection of feathers, pigeon feathers. Mom says they're dirty, but . . ."

"No, it's not feathers. I've got wings."

"You found a whole wing and you picked it up? Oh, YUK!" Angela looked disgusted. "Was there blood on it? Maybe a car hit it and . . . Oh, yuk!"

"NO!" screamed Jennifer. "I've got wings. Here . . . on my back, dodo! Real ones!"

She spun around.

"Jen, are you going nuts or something?"

"No, really! You can't see them. I can't even see them, except in the mirror. But they do all these wing things. They flutter and . . ."

Angela was looking at Jennifer very strangely. She began to back away.

"No, Ange, really!" Desperation was beginning to well up into panic. "Angela!"

Jennifer had to do something. She wiggled her shoulders and prayed for the best. She felt a little flutter on her back and up she rose!

"Angela! Look at me!"

Angela stood rooted to the spot as Jennifer wobbled a foot or so above the ground. She stared until Jennifer thought her eyes were going to pop. "How'd you do that?"

Jennifer landed with a little plop. "I told you," she said miserably, "I've got wings."

"But there's nothing there."

"I guess you can't see them, either."

"You've got invisible wings?" Angela's voice rose disbelievingly. "OK. Do it again."

Jennifer sighed. She was resigned. She fluttered a little, then lifted off the ground on a tilt. "I haven't really got the hang of it yet," she apologized. "It's not as easy as you think."

"Do it again."

Once more Jennifer rose a foot or two. This time she even traveled horizontally for a second before she tipped and stumbled to the floor.

"Ohmagod! You've got wings!"

"That's what I've been trying to tell you!"

"But how did it happen? Where did they come from?" Angela was almost dancing with excitement. "It's the greatest thing that ever happened to anybody! Oh, Jenny, tell me everything! Can you fly? I bet you can fly!" Her eyes were shining as she sprang toward Jennifer, her arms reaching for a hug. But as the arms encircled her, Jennifer gave a little screech of pain.

"You're crushing them! No! Let go!"

Angela sprang back. "Ohmagod, I'm sorry. Are you OK?"

Jennifer nodded and gulped.

"Can I touch them?" she whispered in awe.

"I guess so. Just be careful."

"Where are they?" Angela reached out tentatively toward the air near Jennifer's back.

Jennifer felt a light touch. She held very still, afraid, almost, to breathe. "What does it feel like?" she whispered.

"I don't know. It's so thin, like a piece of silk or something." There was vast wonder in Angela's for once quiet voice. She slowly drew her hand away. "How did it happen?" Her real astonishment was almost frightening. Nothing ever shook Angela.

Jennifer turned around. "I don't know. I just drew a picture of me with these things on my back. When I woke up this morning they were just there."

There was silence. Angela waited. "Well?"

"That's all."

"That's it? The whole thing?"

Jennifer nodded. "What am I going to do?" The words came out in a wail.

"I think it's great! Just wait till Penelope or Samantha sees this! Wow! This is one thing they can't top!"

"No!" Jennifer gripped her arm. "You can't tell anyone!"

"Why not? You told me and I think it's great! If it happened to me, I'd tell everybody!"

"No, you wouldn't. It's too weird."

Angela looked unconvinced.

"Now, look, Angela, you promised! I've got to figure

out what to do first. You promised. Not one teeny, weeny hint to anyone, understand! I haven't even told my mother yet."

"You haven't? You tell your mother everything!"

"I just have to figure things out first, that's all." Jennifer looked at her feet. "I'll tell her."

"You mean I'm the only one who knows? Wow!"

"Now, promise me, Angela. No one!"

"But you'll be famous! Can't you just see yourself in the *Enquirer*? Right next to 'Woman Gives Birth to Two-Headed Snake,' there you'll be: 'Girl Sprouts Wings!' Everyone in line at the supermarket would read it. You could give flying demonstrations!"

"No, Angela. I swear, if anyone finds out, I'll know where they got it from, and I'll kill you. If you ever tell a soul, I'll announce to the whole grade that you like Robert. . . ."

The horrified look in Angela's eyes stopped her. "You wouldn't!"

"I would." Jennifer glowered at her. "I will."

"OK, I won't. I promise, I won't."

"OK, but if anyone we know knows, I'll know where they heard it."

"OK!"

"OK!" They both sounded mad. Then suddenly Angela giggled. "You know, Jen, if this is really going to be a secret, I think we'd better have some kind of code. You know, like naming them or something."

"Naming them? Angela, you are so weird! That's nuts!"

"No, really. Then, if we have to talk about them we can and no one'll know. Instead of saying, 'Hi,

Jen, how are your wings today?,' it'll be, 'Hi, how's so and so?' "

"Well . . ."

"But it would have to be a name no one we know has, like . . . I know . . . who was that guy with the wax wings we were studying? Oh, yeah, Icarus . . . or Daedalus!"

"Icarus?" Jennifer looked at her incredulously. "That's stupid. What do you think people would think if they heard you say, 'How's Icarus today?' "

"Icky, for short."

"Anyway, his wings melted, remember? I'm not crazy about that. He fell into the sea or something and drowned."

"OK. Let me think." She stared into space. "Then it has to be a common name no one we know has." They thought for a second. "I got it! Fred! We don't know a Fred!"

"Fred!" Jennifer was outraged. "Fred? My wings, Fred?"

"Oh, forgodsake, Jen, you don't like anything. Why don't you think of something?"

"OK." Jennifer was gazing into the unknown. If there was one name in the whole world she could have, it would be . . . "Dawn," she said. "I've always loved the name Dawn."

Angela practiced saying it. "How's Dawn today?" she said. "Or . . . Dawn's a little droopy today. Yeah, that sounds great!"

"Shhhhh," Jennifer whispered. There were voices out in the hall.

". . . They'll miss their class. They're probably together."

"They always are, the Bobbsey twins." That was Samantha.

"Do you think they're talking about us?"

Angela put her fingers to her lips and nodded.

". . . get into trouble. Where do you think . . ." The voices grew fainter and then disappeared altogether.

"We'd better get out of here before they call home," hissed Angela. "Let's get Dawn to swimming."

Jennifer's hand went to her mouth in horror. "I can't go to swim."

"Why not? Ducks have wings and they swim."

"They just sit on top of the water and paddle. They don't have to practice the backstroke. My wings . . . Dawn will get all soggy."

"You'd have to hang them out to dry, like a cormorant." She started to giggle at the picture of Jennifer perched on the diving board holding her wings out. Then she caught a glimpse of her face. "OK, I'm sorry. I'll be serious. Look, I know! We'll say you're sick and I've been in the ladies' room with you, OK? Then they'll send you to the nurse and that'll take the whole period."

"But there's nothing wrong with me."

"So what! By the time she finds that out, swim will be over and we'll have all spring vacation to figure out what to do. Trust me. It'll be fine."

"I guess so. How do I look?"

"OK, but your sweater's sort of funny in the back. Turn around and I'll fix it."

"Just be careful. OW!"

"Sorry. I wish I could see them. Tell me if I pull something I shouldn't." Angela started to smooth the sweater over Jennifer's shoulders. "Oh, God, how I wish I could see what they look like! They feel huge!"

"They are. Angela, what does my sweater look like, in the back where I cut into it, I mean. Can you see the holes?"

"Yes, but it's sort of neat. It looks like you're going punk. If you cut a couple of holes in the front and tore it down one arm, it'd look perfect. Want me to try?"

"NO!"

"Just trying to help." She sounded disappointed. "There, that's better. At least it isn't all bunched up on one side. Are you ready?"

"I guess so."

They looked at the door. "Can you hear anything?"

"No, can you?"

Angela opened the door a crack and looked out. "It's clear," she said. "Come on."

The two girls picked up their bookbags and quickly slipped out of the closet. There was no one in the hallway. They nodded at each other, then headed for the nurse's office. "I'll meet you after school," Angela said as they started up the stairs, "under the clock. Then we can decide what to do."

"Just remember," said Jennifer, clutching Angela's arm, "you promised. One word and you're dead meat." She was suddenly sorry she had said anything at all, even to Angela. Especially to Angela.

"I said I wouldn't. Don't worry. Trust me."

Outside the nurse's office they went their separate ways. "See you later, Jen." She squeezed her hand. "Oh, Jen, this is so exciting! I can't stand it!"

Then Jennifer knocked and went in.

A few minutes later she heard Angela's voice outside. "Sick as a dog," she was saying. And Jennifer drew a long sigh of relief.

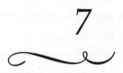

# 7

# On the Way Home

The rest of the school day was almost uneventful. Jennifer sat in the nurse's office for a while and, as usual, the nurse was too busy with a sprained ankle and a broken finger to really examine her. She had to agree that Jennifer didn't look quite right. It was nothing she could put her finger on, but she thought it was best not to take any chances. That took care of swim. When she got back to her class, Angela looked up and tilted her head questioningly. Just the way Cleopatra did, thought Jennifer as she nodded meaningfully at her, except that Angela's eyebrows went up instead of her ears.

She slipped into her seat and put her hand over her stomach and tried to look sick. She was very good at it and it was enough to keep Mr. Gomez from bothering her.

As soon as they took a break Angela wove her way around the desk toward her. "How's Dawn doing?" she asked in a low, conspiratorial voice.

"Who's Dawn?" Samantha leaned over toward them.

Angela and Jennifer looked at each other. Samantha always had to know everything. "A friend of ours . . . from camp," said Jennifer quickly. "You don't know her."

"How do you know? What's her last name?"

Jennifer squirmed. "Twitching," said Angela. "Dawn Twitching."

Jennifer choked.

"Dawn Twitching!" Samantha cracked up. "I don't believe it."

Jennifer caught a glimpse of David's face as he sat down, sprawling over the seat in front of her. He cupped his hands over his mouth and leaned in to whisper something to Samantha. She nodded and glanced back at Jennifer, smirking. Jennifer tried to scrunch lower in her chair. But her wings caught on the back and stopped her. Samantha giggled again. Jennifer turned and threw a dirty look at Angela. "Twitching?" she mouthed.

Angela grimaced and shrugged, looking helpless. "Sorry," she mouthed back.

Then there was only closing assembly to contend with. There was no way she could get out of chorus; she had a couple of lines to sing solo and the music teacher knew she was there. "Not to worry," said Angela, "all you have to do is act natural."

Angela walked right up behind her all the way to the auditorium, covering her back. Jennifer had to sit with the chorus, but they managed to get there early and find an end seat on the side for her. "See ya later," Angela said as she left to sit with their class. Jennifer sat down sideways so her wings could hang down to the floor comfortably. She looked around. No one was paying any attention to her, and she had about an hour before she had to get up to sing.

On stage the teachers and the principal made their speeches. The third-graders played "Kumbaya" on their recorders, the second grade sang "Friendship," and two boys from the sixth grade read from the Old Testament. Jennifer planned her approach to the stage. All she had to do was stay on the side, then stand in the back where no one would really see her.

"And now the chorus will sing 'My Favorite Things.' If the chorus will please come up on stage."

Jennifer got up, her heart pounding. But it really wasn't that bad. She sort of scooted up the aisle with her back to the wall, as if she were looking for someone, then walked up on stage facing the front. The chorus had their eyes glued to Mrs. Krell — all but Jennifer. She ignored Mrs. Krell signaling her to move to the front of the chorus and pretended to be looking for someone in the balcony. They started singing, but a brush of air suddenly swept up under Dawn, and she felt the tips of her wings wobble. She pressed her shoulders down and reached behind her to hold them. Then, suddenly, she was aware of silence; no one was singing and the piano was playing a familiar melody, for the second time? Mrs. Krell was staring right at her. Huh? Oh, it's my line, she thought, and jumped in: "Roses of kittens," she heard herself sing out, "Noses like mittens." A couple of kids looked up. Someone behind her snickered. Jennifer rolled her eyes, stared straight ahead, and kept singing.

When it was over she edged back against the wall to her seat and sat, perched, ready for flight. Heather turned around and looked at her. "Noses like mittens?"

she mouthed. "What happened to you?" Jennifer shrugged, then reached down to get one of the wings unstuck. It was caught in the seat.

On stage the principal was talking again. "I know you're anxious to stay here." There was a loud groan from the kids. "But" — Jennifer tensed and yanked at the wing; she had to get out of there fast — "I must sorrowfully announce that you are officially on . . . vacation!" The kids sprang up, cheering, and surged toward the aisle. But Jennifer was ready. She leaped up, then scurried up the aisle barely ahead of the mob, conscious of her wings slapping urgently against her legs. The kids were catching up. She didn't want her wings crushed, so she went faster. In the hallway she pressed herself against the wall as the swarms pushed their way out through the doors and rushed past. She waited until the halls were quiet, then ducked up the stairs, grabbed her things, and headed out to meet Angela.

" 'Twitching'!" she shrieked.

"Well, it was the only thing I could think of. It just sort of popped out. Are you OK?"

"I guess so."

"What took you so long?"

"I was afraid of getting crushed, so I waited. Anyway, I walk funny. I feel like a penguin." She made her sick duck face. "Maybe when I get used to them it'll be easier." She looked hopeful.

"Ya. Don't worry about it. This is only your first day with the . . . I mean, with Dawn." They had started walking. "What do you want to do now? Do you want to go anywhere special?"

"I don't know." As they walked by the construction site across the street from school, one of the workmen

· 53 ·

stopped shoveling as they passed. He leaned on his shovel, waiting for them to go by. "I just want to go somewhere where I don't have to talk with anyone and I can think."

There was a gust of wind and Jennifer felt a sudden release on her back. Her body swung forward. She fought for control.

Up she rose. It was only an inch or two above the ground, but she could feel herself being lifted. She tried to press her wings down again against the enormous pressure of the little puffs of air. Her feet churned, thrashing and kicking as the sand whirled under her. She forced herself to concentrate, struggling against an invisible energy. She had to stop! The sand was flying now, her arms were flailing and her feet scrabbling frantically for a foothold. She clenched her eyes shut and strained.

Then the gust passed and her wings suddenly snapped shut. She dropped, pitched forward, and lay sprawled on the pile of dirt now drifting gently down around her.

She looked up, finally, to see Angela standing over her, openmouthed. The construction worker was still leaning on his shovel, rooted to the spot and staring. She blinked once or twice, then sat up.

At her movement they all seemed to come to life. Angela rushed forward. "Are you all right?"

"I . . . I think so." She tentatively stretched out one leg, then the other. Then she scrambled to her feet and started to brush herself off. She almost tripped over a wing. "I . . . I guess so. Oh, look at me!" She pounded at her skirt. Billows of red sand rose around her.

Behind the cloud of dust the construction worker sputtered. "What the hell was that?"

Jennifer shrank back. "I . . . I . . ." She looked desperately at Angela.

"Was what?" Angela was fully recovered now. Her voice was full of innocence.

"What? That. That . . . that dance?"

"What dance? Oh, that!" She thought fast. "Oh, that's called the Sand Shuffle. We do it at my country house all the time. Wanna see it again?"

"Let's get out of here," hissed Jennifer, reaching down for her backpack.

But Angela was standing in the middle of the mound of sand doing the soft-shoe routine they'd done in their class play the year before. Little puffs of dust were rising again. Jennifer grabbed her arm and pulled. Angela danced off, waving. "She does it better than I do!" she called. Then they turned and fled.

Jennifer hurried down the block lugging her backpack and feeling her wings flopping against her again. It felt almost normal. At the corner they had to wait for the light to change. They turned to look back at the construction site. The man was still watching them, shaking his head and kicking at the ground as if he were trying to figure it out. And behind him were a few kids walking their way. "Oh, no, what if they saw that!" Jennifer realized that she was trembling.

"They didn't see a thing," said Angela, "but I can see where this might be a problem." Then she started to giggle. "Ohmagod! You should have seen what you looked like! And that man! He . . . he couldn't believe it!" The giggles were growing. "You should have seen his face when you went UP!" The laughter poured out, now, and she leaned back against the building, laughing helplessly. Even Jennifer felt a little giggle rising.

"And," she howled, "did you see all that sand flying? And when you went into that dance!" She had to gasp for breath. "Oh, my God!"

The whole ridiculous picture suddenly hit Jennifer and her giggles began to erupt. Then she felt the breeze. "Oh, no!" The wings stirred on her back. "Ange! It's going to happen again!"

Angela opened her eyes and saw a glimpse of pure terror.

"There are too many people . . . Angela!"

Angela grabbed her, then, holding Jennifer with one hand, she leaned over to pick up their things with the other.

"Please, Ange, hold me down if I start to go up!" Jennifer clutched at Angela's arm as she felt a fresh breeze stir her.

"OK, now." As usual Angela took charge. "You hold on to me on this side and your backpack will be like a weight on the other." They shifted around, weighing her down as well as they could. "Here, take this. Now, how does that feel?"

"OK."

"Just turn a little and, oh, there's the bus! Let's GO!" They hobbled across the avenue, Jennifer holding on to Angela as tightly as she could. She could feel the air pulling at her. As they staggered across, Angela waved madly at the driver and he opened the door.

They knew it was a mistake the second they got on, but it was too late. The bus was jammed and kids were already pushing on behind them.

"Just stay behind me," Jennifer pleaded to Angela.

She had never really been aware of space before. In fact, she had always been a part of the bus crush. It was fun to push and be caught and shove and scream to be heard. Somehow it had made her feel as if she were a part of the group. Not now.

"Ow!" She felt her wing caught by something behind her. Someone scraped by and jabbed an elbow into her side. "Get off or you're dead meat."

She backed up against Angela even further, trying to protect her wings, and felt them crunch against her back. She put her arms down, her hands flat against Dawn, pressing them close to her body, trying to keep her balance as the bus rocked along. The bus lurched and swerved. Angela lost her balance, swung in over the seats, then swung out again and was gone. Jennifer suddenly found herself staring at the zipper of a strange, green backpack. "Angela?" Jennifer turned her head and her nose squashed against the button of a tweed jacket.

"Move to the rear! Folks, there's plenty of room back there," the bus driver called. "Move it!" The tweed jacket shuffled forward an inch and Jennifer, trapped, shuffled with it.

The doors opened again and more kids pushed on. Wedged between the backpack and the jacket, Jennifer hobbled a few more steps with them as they were squashed from behind. Then, over a shoulder and under an arm, she caught a glimpse of Angela's worried eyes searching for her. Their eyes linked. Silent questions and hopeless shrugs traveled the small space between them. Then someone shifted and Angela disappeared again.

Jennifer stood, trapped, and endured. She stood with

her hands at her sides, holding her wings close against her as she swayed with the lurching of the bus. She didn't dare move, even when someone reached over her head to pour potato chips down another kid's shirt and the spray of chips showered down over them all. She knew that one had landed in her hair, but she couldn't even reach up to brush it off. She looked up. There was one big chip sitting stationary, midair above her. She didn't even want to know about the other one caught in her wings.

Then, between bodies, she saw Samantha and Kathy. They were staring at her. Oh, no.

Samantha giggled and pointed at her. Then she covered her mouth and whispered something to Kathy. Jennifer was sure that she heard a muffled giggle over the din as Kathy's head nodded up and down behind the cupped hand.

"How's Dawn Twitching?" Samantha's voice sailed sweetly across the bus. Jennifer turned away and stared at the green backpack. She felt as if she could hardly breathe. Ohmagod, what if she got sick right there?

The ride was interminable. Jennifer knew it was never going to end. She'd be squished there for the rest of her life, suffocating, careening from side to side as the bus rocked its way down the street, and listening to Samantha's snicker. Then, suddenly, miraculously, finally, a bunch of kids pushed their way off. They crushed her wings with their backpacks as they squeezed by but she didn't care. She found herself standing by herself in the wide aisle of the bus, Angela's worried eyes peering into hers. Even Samantha and Kathy were gone.

"Come on," Angela said. And when the doors opened, Jennifer let herself be led down the steps. The doors sprung closed. "Ohmagod!" She leaped as they snapped shut behind her. She stood on the sidewalk staring after the bus. One more second and Dawn would have been caught. She could just picture the bus chugging on down the street, her wings caught in the door and the rest of her hanging out.

"I can't believe it," she stammered.

Angela was leaning in toward her anxiously. "Are you all right? How's Dawn?" Angela was brushing the potato chips out of her hair. A sprinkle of crumbs showered out around her.

"I don't know." She could feel the wings fluttering on her back. Were they trembling all by themselves or was she? "Nothing hurts. What does it look like back there?" she asked as Angela straightened her sweater.

"It's OK." Angela examined her back more closely. "Your sweater's torn, but I can't see anything else."

Jennifer groaned. What would her mother say? She felt a long sigh escape from deep inside her. She was suddenly weak. "Let's go home, Ange. I want to go home." She felt a little gust of wind catch the tip of her wing. "Whoops! Oh, no."

Angela grabbed her sweater and pulled her back. "Let's just get there before anything else happens. We've got to figure out how to control these things."

By the time they reached Jennifer's house they had worked out a walking technique. Each time a wind gusted up, Angela merely hopped close behind Jennifer to keep it from coming up under the wings. The girls hugged the buildings, zigzagging their way across the street. They looked kind of strange, they thought. But no one really paid any attention to two kids fooling around. They were supposed to act like that.

"Are they fun?"

"How do I know? I haven't had a chance to find out yet."

The two girls were sprawled out on Jennifer's bed. For the first time all day Jennifer could relax, and it felt wonderful.

"I don't even know how to make them work right." Jennifer grinned, then grimaced. "So far they're just a real pain."

She took another Oreo, twisted it open, and inspected the white, sugary layer. It was perfect. She licked it with the tip of her tongue, then looked at the inroad she had made. She liked to make pictures on Oreos. She was developing it into a fine art. Angela, on the other hand, chomped down on the whole cookie and demolished it in two bites. Chocolate and sugar crushed into each other and crumbs sprayed down over the flowered comforter. Angela swiped at them but they just sort of bounced on the bed covers and lay there. She licked the tips of her fingers and pressed one fingertip into the crumbs. Then she licked them off her finger thoughtfully.

"That bus was the pits."

"I've got to remember to get off the front," Jennifer said gloomily. Then suddenly she remembered the sailing hop that had saved her from the doors and those few moments of lightness and buoyancy as the wind breezed up under her and she had lifted. They were brief hints of how she could feel.

Angela reached for another Oreo. "You know," she

said carefully, sneaking a look at Jennifer's face, "I bet you really could fly." She paused, waiting. "I mean really fly, not just little hops. We have to find a way to try it in something bigger than a closet."

"I don't know. If I did try it I would need space to figure it all out."

"You could always open the window and zoom out."

"Smooth, Angela. I'd probably kill myself."

"Just kidding."

They were silent for a while and then suddenly Angela sat up straight. "I know!" she exclaimed. "The Rink!"

# 8

## Trying Dawn Out

Angela and Jennifer ran up the stairs to The Rink and pushed open the door. They peeked around it. No one was there; no one but Scott and Don.

Don looked up from his crossword puzzle. "You girls have a lesson today?"

"No, but can we skate if no one else shows up?"

Don shrugged lazily. "Getting conscientious, aren't you?" They looked at him, waiting. "Sure, you can skate. That's five bucks apiece."

"Just put it on the account."

This time he looked at them more closely. "Are you sure your mothers know you're having this extra time?"

"Don't worry, it's fine. They'll be thrilled we want to practice more. Trust me. Really."

Don looked at them skeptically. They stood before his desk, a little flushed, a gleam in their eyes, their skates over their shoulders.

"Well, OK. But . . ."

But they'd already hurried to the benches and flung

their bags on the floor. They shrugged off their sweaters and tore off their shoes, one toe pushing at the heel of the other. A shoe popped off and skidded across the room.

"Just pray that nobody else comes," muttered Angela under her breath as they bent over to put on their skates.

"What about them?" Jennifer nodded toward the two men at the desk. Scott was absorbed in a book. He hadn't even looked up. And Don was leaning over his crossword puzzle. He heaved a sigh and slowly unraveled himself from his seat. He ambled toward them, shoe in hand.

"Girls, aren't you old enough to take care of your things? Here, do something with this." He held it out. "I'd hate to think what your rooms look like." They stared up at him.

"Don't you girls have school?"

"Vacation," murmured one, pulling at her laces.

"We're off," the other muttered as she pushed her foot into the boot.

Angela bent over to lace up her boot. "Fuffm brugh the afht," her muffled voice explained.

"Sure," he shrugged and ambled on toward the back room.

Jennifer let out her breath and Angela looked up and giggled.

"What did you say?" asked Jennifer.

"I don't know. 'Fluff, bunf, munf,' or something." She giggled again and took off her lavender blade booties. The clock on the far wall showed five minutes to go till their ice time. They were still the only people there.

Don glanced up from his puzzle. "You girls can go on if you want," he said. "I don't think anyone else is going to show."

On the ice they started their warm-up. They always did the same routine: first forward skating, then cross-overs, then the backward crossovers. Around and around they skated. "OK," Angela said as she caught up to Jennifer. "Just like we planned. I'll be the lookout."

Jennifer glanced around. There was still no one there. Her heart was beating very fast. "Just make sure you tell me if you see anyone. Angela, if anyone comes . . ."

"Don't worry! Trust me." She sounded surprised and hurt.

They stole a furtive look in the direction of the men.

"What do you think?" Angela's voice was excited as they swung into the middle of the rink. "Are you ready?"

"I'm nervous. Is anyone looking?"

Angela squinted and peered out into the lounge. There was no one in sight; Scott was bent over his book. Nothing was going to tear him away. He flipped a page and kept reading. Don had disappeared altogether.

"Now. Do it now!"

"You're sure?"

"Positive! Come on, Jen, do something. Anything!"

Tentatively Jennifer opened her wings. They rose up around her. She could feel them. Almost as if she were afraid to look, she lifted her eyes toward the mirrors.

And heard a gasp behind her.

"Oh, Jen, they're beautiful!"

There they were, towering above her, catching the

light of the ice. Wiry and silvery strings reflected the light here and there like a spider's web filled with dew, catching the sunlight. Jennifer was stunned. She had never dreamed they could be so beautiful. Instinctively she took a step toward them and suddenly felt the air rush under them. The one little movement carried her sailing across the ice. Her wings fanned out behind her as she glided effortlessly toward herself. She saw herself, not in the old, faded blue jeans that were too short, and not in the crinkled blue sweater, its yarn unraveling as she glided, but in white tulle, sprinkled with sparkling snow: a snow maiden, a *Nutcracker* snowflake.

Then she heard a warning screech. "Jennifer!" And she was in blue jeans again and her image was coming up too fast.

Frantically she tried to press her wings down. They jerked convulsively as she skidded toward the mirror. Her skates sputtered as she tried to stop. She put out her hands and met herself, hand to hand, knee to knee. She slid down the mirrored wall and onto the ice. She lay on her stomach for a moment. Then, as Angela raced toward her, she lifted her head. Her eyes were shining.

"Are you all right? How did it feel?"

"It was wonderful!" Jennifer gasped. "How did it look?"

"It was great till the end. I don't think you've really got the hang of it yet."

"No one saw, did they?" She turned over and sat up.

"I don't think so."

Jennifer jumped. "Think?"

"I mean, no." Angela flew to the windows and peered

out. There was only Scott, still hunched over his book.

"Try it again. But this time control it."

Jennifer faced the mirror. She pressed her shoulders down slowly. Her wings lowered behind her. She let them up again until they just peered out a bit from her sides, then lowered them. She brought them out halfway, then fully, as her confidence grew. Standing as still as she could, she tried variations of the full wing, then the flutter and the sweep. She went into various combinations. Without the threat of a breeze, her wings lowered and raised obediently. She stood very still, sure that nothing moved but Dawn. Mesmerized by them, she felt as if time had disappeared. There was nothing; nothing except the wings that moved in so many ways. Up and down they lifted in great sweeping arches. They rippled and quivered, then rose around her as if they were petals. She brought them out fully and let go. She moved.

She felt herself sailing. She circled and circled, picking up speed, feeling her wings streaming out behind her, feeling the new sensations that pressed under her and took her forward. She felt as if she could lift.

But she was afraid to. Consciously and deliberately she lowered her wings and came to a full stop. She hardly dared to move, not wanting to leave those sensations behind.

"Oh, Jen," Angela breathed. "Oh, Jen."

The girls gazed at the wings in the mirror and then one of them drew a sigh that brought them back to reality.

"Oh, Jen, that was fabulous! Try it again! Try something else! Do something! Can you believe what your jumps are going to be like?"

"Jumps?"

"Please? Just a little one?"

"I'm not sure."

"Oh, come on. Try it. We don't have much time." They looked out into the lounge. Scott was bent over, putting on his skates. Don was still out of sight. Jennifer was skeptical. "Please. It'll be fine. Believe me."

Jennifer could feel herself wavering. The memory of her last sail was too wonderful not to want it again.

She glided across the ice, just feeling her wings for a moment or two, then began. Her heart was beating quickly, her skates skimming the surface. She struggled to keep her wings down until she had picked up a little speed, then she bent her gliding knee in preparation for the jump. She opened her wings and took a tentative hop.

The lift was terrific!

She felt herself carried up and out over the ice. Angela was staring up at her. "Land!" she screeched, "land!" But Jennifer couldn't. She was midair and traveling. The wall was coming up at her.

"I can't turn!" She tried to tip but somehow her wings were not coordinated with the rest of her. And as they flailed, the edge of her blade caught the ice and she felt the whole white world coming up at her.

When she opened her eyes she found herself staring up at the silver foil ceiling. Then Angela's worried face intervened, and the white glow overhead disappeared.

"Are you all right?" she said for the fourth time that day.

Jennifer nodded, unable to speak. Her breaths were coming out in small, mewing gasps.

"Ohmagod, ohmagod," was all that came out. Then, " 'Just a little one,' huh?" when she could finally speak.

They heard the door to the rink creak open. Scott was framed in the doorway looking out across the ice. He started out, limping, one skate on, the other in his hand. "Are you OK?"

"Stop him!" Jennifer gasped.

Angela nodded. "She just took a flop." Then, to Jennifer, "You're fine, right?" Jennifer nodded and waved a hand at him weakly. When the door closed behind Scott, Angela let her breath out slowly. "That was a close one. I guess you'd better practice."

"Yeah." She picked herself up off the ice.

"Do you want to try it again?"

"No!"

A few minutes later they were finishing their hot chocolate. "I guess it'll take a lot of control," Jennifer said. "Just a wiggle would do for a jump like that."

They were hunting under the benches for their shoes when Penelope came in. She headed for a bench and pulled off her shoes.

"You have a lesson?" Jennifer asked.

"Uh huh. Did you?"

"No. We just came in to practice."

"Really?" Penelope looked a little shy. "Gee, I . . . if you want to practice again sometime, maybe we could go together."

Angela gave Jennifer a little warning nudge. "Yeah . . . sure. Well, we have to go." They brushed past her on their way to the door. "See ya."

"Sure." She finished lacing up her skates, looked at them for a moment, then headed out to the ice.

At the door Jennifer hung back for a moment. Penelope was practicing something new, circling the ice, using the whole rink for her crossovers. She did a three turn, then took off, turning in midair, as if she were doing a backward waltz jump. She missed her edge on the landing and went down. She sat on the ice, her head in her hands for a moment, then rose and started again, faster now. Up she went and down again, sliding to the ice. She slapped the snow off her tights as she stood up and began again. Don stirred as a new crash shook the glass. "She's down again?"

Jennifer nodded.

"She'll get it." He stretched and yawned, then leaned back in his chair. "That's the way she does everything. Good kid."

"Come on, Jen," Angela called. Penelope was beginning to circle the ice again. Jennifer saw her glance out at them as Angela swung open the door. Even if she wanted to, now she couldn't go skating with Penelope. Suddenly Jennifer felt terrible.

They were halfway down the flight of steps before Angela spoke. "I really think you need some practice with Dawn," she said slowly, "somewhere where there's loads of room."

Jennifer stopped on the stairs. She felt herself stiffen. "Is this going to be one of your fatal ideas?"

"I think you ought to fly."

# 9

# *Wing Covers*

Dinner was over and the two girls were sprawled out over Jennifer's bed again. Jennifer had been sure that dinner would be nerve-racking, but it had gone better than she had thought it would. She usually resented it when her mother was preoccupied with work, but tonight it was a mitzvah. And her wings had hardly gotten in the way at all. At the table Jennifer had been very careful to sit with them flowing up and over the back of her chair.

"You certainly are sitting up straight, sweetheart," her mother had commented as she glanced up. The two girls had thrown sideways glances toward each other.

"Mom, you know how important good posture is."

Her mother had looked at her disbelievingly. "Are you sure you're my daughter? The one who slumps and sits on her knees . . . sideways?"

Jennifer heard a little snort from Angela. She threw an angry look her way.

"Well, Scott says that my spins'll be better if I'm

straighter. Did you know that your stomach has to be flat against your spine?" She sucked her breath in and thought thin.

"Oh, honey, how could you spin in that position? It looks sort of awkward. Don't you have to breathe?"

"I can breathe." Her voice was tight with the effort. "This is the way it's supposed to be."

Angela leaped to her feet. "Except that your shoulders go up when you hold in your stomach. See, your shoulders have to go down and your elbows have to go up. Your stomach is in and your hips are tucked under. See, it's easy."

Jennifer's mother giggled. "Somehow I don't think that's what Scott had in mind. You look like a couple of anorexic penguins with stomachaches. But, Angela, since you're already standing, why don't you clear the table, if you can walk like that. You, too, Jen. Then take dessert into your room. I have to get back to work as soon as the dishes are done."

They scooped out mounds of chocolate chip mint ice cream and disappeared into Jennifer's room.

"The thing is," said Angela, as she bit into the ice cream, "the mirrors."

"What are you talking about?"

"Dawn."

Jennifer sighed. She was beginning to get tired of talking or even thinking about Dawn. "Well, what is it?"

"The thing is, if I can see Dawn in the mirrors, then everyone else can, too. Right?"

"I guess so." Uncertainty was growing again.

"So the logical thing is to cover them."

"I can't cover every mirror in the world, Angela. That's dumb."

"You mean like Dracula?" Angela giggled. "No, dodo, not the mirrors, your wings!"

"Oh, smooth. Can't you see me walking down the street with some weird things sticking out of my back?" Jennifer was disgusted.

"You could say you were going to a costume party!" The look on Jennifer's face stopped her. "That was a joke, Jen. Well, anyway, you don't need them on the street. I mean, there are hardly any mirrors there. The real problem is the rink." Jennifer looked up quickly. "There are mirrors all over the place. And we won't always be the only ones there. And what about your lessons? And the test? And what if I'm sick or something . . . or late? I can't just always be there to be the lookout."

Jennifer looked doubtful. "So?"

"Well, I've got it all figured out."

"Uh oh."

"Oh, forgodsake, Jen, don't be so suspicious. The thing is, you don't just walk into Bloomingdale's and say, 'In what department do you carry wing covers, please?' "

"So?"

"So, we make them!" Her voice had a triumphant ring to it.

"Make them? How? We've never made anything."

"Sure we have. Just think of all those Barbie doll costumes. We'll just think of you as a giant Barbie doll."

"It's not the same, Angela."

Angela ignored her. "And you'll say they're part of your skating costume! And that you have to practice with them on to get used to them!" Angela was getting excited as she improvised. "That's it! All you have to do is skate to a song with 'wings' in it and you've got it made! Well?" There was that triumphant ring again.

Jennifer paused as she thought about it. "Well, I guess it could work, but . . ."

"Think of some wing songs. I bet there's loads of them." She was already rummaging around Jennifer's desk drawer for a pencil. "I'll make a list."

"Well, my mother's always singing some song about a snow white dove."

"Great." She wrote it down. "What else?"

"There's 'Broken Wings.' "

"Mmmmmmm. 'Broken Wings,' " Angela repeated as she wrote. "I'm not sure I'd want that one. What else?"

"There's that song from *Peter Pan*, 'I'm Flying.' " Five or six more titles were scribbled down. "OK, at least we know we have plenty to pick from. Now, all we have to do is make the wing covers."

"That's ALL?" Jennifer was definitely worried.

"I told you, I've got it all figured out. Where's a Barbie doll? Let me show you." Reluctantly, Jennifer dug into one of her drawers and pulled out a bedraggled Barbie. She handed it to Angela. "See, pretend this is you. Now pretend there are wings coming off her back, OK? Got it?" Jennifer nodded dubiously. Angela grabbed a sock off the floor. "See, we wrap it around the wing like this and leave a little tail hanging off the edges, for effect." She glanced at the expression on Jennifer's face. "It'll be beautiful. Trust me."

Jennifer stared at the sock sticking out of the back of the Barbie doll. "That looks ridiculous."

"Well, can you think of anything better?"

"It looks like an Egyptian mummy."

"Jennifer, we're not going to use a sock! We'll get

something really nice. It's the principle that I'm talking about."

"Well, what can we use?"

Angela looked at her sideways. "Well," she said slowly, "I don't know. What about something from your costume drawer?"

"Oh, Angela, no!" Jennifer looked stricken. But Angela was already opening the drawer and digging in.

It was a jumble of satins and velvets, old scarves and sheets, stuffed in and tangled together. This drawer had been the center of Jennifer's fantasy life for as long as she could remember.

"Let's see what you've got in here." Angela reached in, dumped it out onto the floor, and began to go through it. At the bottom of the pile a tiny sliver of pink satin peeped out. Angela pulled at it and drew out a pink chiffon negligee.

"That's it," she breathed. "It's perfect."

"Oh, no!"

It had been the princess's train and the bride's veil. It had been the queen's robes. It had been fairy wings; it had been all the elegant, beautiful, delicate things.

"Trust me. It's perfect."

Jennifer felt tears forming behind her eyes. It had always made her feel magical. If they cut it up she'd probably never feel that way again.

Angela looked up at her. "Oh, Jen, I'm sorry. Maybe we can think of something else." She rummaged in the pile again and came up with a sheet. It had big blue and yellow flowers all over it — bright blue and yellow. They'd never wear that in the Ice Capades.

"Any other ideas?"

Jennifer shrugged. Angela tried again. "Do you have any money? Maybe we could buy something."

Jennifer shook her head. She rubbed the delicate chiffon between her fingers. She had always loved the feel of it; so soft and light. She tried to think of what it would look like on the rink, sailing out behind her or twirling around her in a spin.

A little smile touched her face. She sighed deeply and let it go. "OK," she succumbed, "let's do it."

Fifteen minutes later her beautiful pink chiffon was in pieces. It didn't exactly look as they had pictured it would. The pieces lay tattered and sad and shapeless, little heaps on the floor. Jennifer gazed at them dismally.

"Now what?"

Angela stirred. "Well, now all we have to do is make them." But her voice was lacking its usual cheerful ring. "Believe me, it won't be as bad as you think."

Jennifer stared at the limp wisps of fabric straggling over the rug. She fingered a tiny scrap of it. Cleopatra looked up and tilted her head. Her tail thumped reassuringly on the floor. "It was so beautiful," Jennifer said softly. Then suddenly, she turned on Angela. "Look at it!" she screamed. "This was your brilliant idea! Just look at it!"

Angela looked. She leaped to her feet. "It's gonna be great! You'll see!"

"Great? Great? It's rags!"

"Jennifer, trust me. I know what I'm doing. Besides, you're the one with the wings. You're the one who said, 'Let's do it,' not me. It was just my idea."

"It sure was."

Angela swiped one of the rags off the floor and held

it up. It was so big she could hardly reach both ends of it.

"At least try it. If it doesn't work . . ."

"It won't."

"It will!" They glared at each other again.

Then Jennifer said, "Do you really think it will?" Her voice was sullen and low but it was enough for Angela. She leaped forward.

"Sure! Now, you stand there," she directed as she pulled Jennifer to the mirror, "so I can see Dawn." Reluctantly Jennifer stared at herself. "Now, put them out."

Jennifer raised the wings and eyed them resentfully as they towered above her. "Now what!"

"Let's see . . ." Angela was thinking. The enormous diaphanous rectangle dripped over her arm. Standing on tiptoe she stretched to reach the tip of the wing. She didn't even come close.

She stepped back and nodded: it was a matter of distance, purely scientific. She took the fabric in hand, calculated the distance to the tip of the wing, and flung it upward. It had barely left her fingers before it floated down and fell gently over Cleopatra's back. There was a flicker of interest in the dog's eyes. Under the pink veil her tail thumped happily.

"Oh, forgodsake," muttered Jennifer.

"Not to worry. It's just a question of thrust and distance." Angela swiped the fabric off Cleo's back, measured the distance, gauged the angle, and took a few practice shots.

"Will you hurry up."

She tossed the pink chiffon as if she were making a basket. This time Cleo snapped at it as it floated back.

"No, Cleo, go away." Angela snatched the fabric

off the floor and hurled it with all her force. It gently wafted down again. "Zilch." She stood back, fed up. "Well, we could always wrap Dawn in Saran Wrap." She giggled suddenly. "Can you just see us trying to peel it off?"

"What if you stood on a chair?"

"Won't work. Then I couldn't see them in the mirror. I know . . . what if you lowered Dawn out to the sides?"

Jennifer lowered her wings to half-mast and in a second felt the weightless fabric slip lightly over her right wing. It was like a brush of air.

"It's working!" Angela sang out in delight.

She felt Angela pinch the cloth together at the base of her wing. "Now, hold still. I'm going to try to pin it." And muttering to herself, she began.

It took a long time, longer than they had thought it would. The fabric was so slippery that it kept sliding around as Angela pinched and pinned. Once or twice she missed the fabric and stuck the pin into Dawn instead. Then it slithered over the wing and dribbled toward the floor. "Oh, for pete's sake." Angela yanked it back into position. It flopped over the other side.

Jennifer groaned. "Hurry." It was beginning to be agony. The wings drooped heavily and her back was beginning to burn. "I can't hold them up there much longer!"

"Don't move! I'm almost there."

"Hurry!"

Then, suddenly, one long wing was covered with floating chiffon. It wrapped around it and then flowed off in a kind of spine. Angela put in the last pin and stood back. "What do you think?"

In the mirror they could see one iridescent, shimmering, nearly transparent wing and one huge, pink, flowing, draped one. "It's great," said Jennifer and lowered her wings with a little sigh of relief.

The second wing went much faster, now that Angela had the hang of it. The end result, they thought, was amazing. Great, pink robes hung out from either side of Jennifer's back. When she put on her skates and stood back to look at the whole effect, she felt a little silly.

"I'm not sure. I think they're too big."

"Just wait till they're all sewn up and you can try them out. I can take off a little here and there. I told you they'd be perfect. Let's see what they look like. Do something."

And Jennifer moved them upward. They fanned out around her. "Wow!" they said.

"Angela!" Jennifer's mother's voice floated in from the other room. "It's nine o'clock. Your mother's waiting for you downstairs."

"OK, Mrs. Rosen." She turned to Jennifer as she grabbed her things and headed out. "Gotta go. Don't worry, they're just great. See ya tomorrow. Call me."

It wasn't until Jennifer had gone back to the mirror that she realized something.

"Angela! Get me out of these things!"

But it was too late. Angela had gone.

# 10

# *Responsibilities*

Jennifer woke trying to remember a dream she had had — something about a butterfly on roller skates — but it was tucked away somewhere out of reach. She unfolded her legs and stretched them out. Her sheets were all tangled, as usual, and she pushed her feet through to the cool air. The sheet was tickling her leg, and sleepily she reached down to scratch. She felt something there; something gauzy and stiff and fine.

Then she remembered.

"Ohmagod."

She was almost afraid to get out of bed, to go to the mirror. But she had to. She almost tripped over pieces of pink chiffon that lay in a heap by her bed, and staggered to the mirror. The wings were dragging, drooping as if they, too, were half asleep. But they were there. She sort of shrugged one shoulder and watched that wing shrug, too. "Wow." Then she turned away and sat down on the edge of her bed. Well, at least there was no school.

She looked around her. Her room, as usual, was a

mess. And this was Saturday — laundry day, cleaning day — the day that the housework had to get done. And she had nothing to wear. The shirt she'd worn yesterday was wrinkled and dirty. She couldn't wear that again. She'd just have to cut up another shirt. But then, when they did the laundry her mother would find the holes.

The picture filled her mind: the laundry room, her mother shaking out the shirts from the dryer, seeing the holes in shirt after shirt. And her sweater! With the wool unraveling until the back was one big hole. And her mother, incredulous and then furious, and all the explanations and the lies she'd have to make up! Or, if she told her mother about the wings, the doctor, and then amputation.

She shook the picture of the operating room out of her mind and dove back into bed. She couldn't allow that to happen.

This was getting so complicated! She'd have to cut up her clothes and then hem them. And do her own laundry. Then she'd have to put it all away and, oh, no, she'd have to learn how to iron.

She tried to think of a way out. Maybe she could say she was going punk. But her mother's voice came through loud and clear, "Not in my house, you don't!"

From the kitchen she could hear rattling noises; that meant her mother was up. She forced herself off the bed. She sighed and marched herself to the kitchen, her wings slapping against her calves with each step. Her mother was sitting at the table staring out the window, coffee cup in hand. Her drawings were spread out over the table before her. She looked bleary. "Hi, sweetheart. Sleep well?"

Jennifer opened the refrigerator and took out some

orange juice, went to the cupboard for the glass, brought it to the table, and slipped onto her chair; all without turning her back to her mother. She felt as if she were doing some weird dance.

"Still practicing good posture?"

"Mmmmm," she nodded as she took a long drink of juice and reached for a bagel. It was the "works," the kind with garlic and salt and onion and sesame seeds. Her mother walked the dog down to the bagel store every Saturday morning and brought them back for breakfast. Sometimes on special occasions they had plain bagels with moist, pink slices of Nova Scotia salmon, cream cheese, slices of tomato, and thin pieces of onion. Today there was just plain cream cheese.

"Mom." Jennifer hoped that her voice sounded nonchalant. "Mom . . ."

"What is it, baby?" Her mother looked up from her coffee. In the mornings she always looked as if she were in a daze, thank goodness.

"Can I ask you something?"

"Sure."

"Ummm . . . I . . . can you teach me how to iron?"

Her mother put down her cup. "Teach you what?"

"Ironing."

"That's what I thought you said. You?"

"Yes." Jennifer thought that some explanation was called for. "Well, you know I'm eleven now . . . almost twelve."

"Yes, I know." She waited.

"And I think it's time I took on some responsibility in the house." There was a long pause.

"You do?"

Jennifer took another bite of her bagel and stared at it. "Mmm hmmm."

"You know, Jen, I think that thought has been expressed before. But I don't think it was you who expressed it. Come here." She opened her arms.

Jennifer looked at her but didn't move. She took another bite and stared at the crumbs that fell. It was usually so nice, sitting on her mother's lap, her arms around her while they talked things over. But she remembered just in time. Jennifer's eyes clouded for a moment. She hadn't thought of that. How could she ever get a hug again? She'd never sit on her mother's lap again. In the mornings her mother couldn't give her a backrub as she woke her for school. Jennifer would have to get up even earlier. Maybe she should tell her.

The operating room loomed again.

Miserably, she sidled away and went back to the refrigerator for another glass of juice. She had to force herself to finish the first glass on the way.

"That's nice," she said, pointing at a drawing on the table.

"Thanks, sweetheart." But there was a question in her mother's voice. Jennifer glanced up, then averted her eyes.

"Anyway, Mom, I think I should do my own ironing from now on. So I want you to teach me."

"Well, OK." Her mother was looking at her as if she were measuring something inside of her daughter. Then she sighed. Jennifer felt a breath run through her, as if she had climbed over the top of some mountain and realized she could get down the other side. "I guess you have to grow up sometime. But I hope you realize that ironing is my favorite thing, that and defrosting the refrigerator." She smiled. "Are you sure you don't want to do that, too?"

Jennifer shook her head. "No, just the ironing."

"Oh." She sounded disappointed. "OK, Jen, when do you want your first lesson?"

"Can you do it now? I need my pink flowered blouse today."

"That's an awfully big thing for you to tackle, Jen. The sleeves and the collar are hard. Why don't we do handkerchiefs."

Handkerchiefs! She couldn't wear a handkerchief! "Mom, I don't even have a handkerchief. Nobody has those anymore."

"Then how about a pillowcase? That's flat."

She thought she was going to scream. She leaned forward desperately. "I don't want to do a pillowcase. Oh, Mom, please, just show me how. I bet I can do it."

Again her mother sighed. "Oh, all right. You get the clothes and I'll get the ironing board. But can I finish my coffee first?"

An hour later Jennifer had ironed her first blouse. It was a little wrinkled in places and scorched here and there, but she had done it herself. Twenty minutes later there was another one and another and another. Her back ached and her hand hurt where a little series of red burns showed. But she had done it.

Her mother was amazed. It was only when she had tried to hug her daughter and Jennifer stepped back that the puzzled, hurt expression crossed over her face.

"I'll put them away. Thanks, Mom," Jennifer said hurriedly, and flinging them over her arm, she ran to her room and closed the door.

She hung the shirts on the doorknob and sat down to cut out the pattern for her wings. In another hour every shirt had two long slits up the back and they were hung in a pastel row. A couple of sweaters were also cut, folded, and put back into their drawers. She changed the sheets on her bed, cleaned up her desk, and put the pieces of Careers and Scrabble into their boxes. The boxes were stacked neatly on the shelf with the other games.

She looked around in satisfaction. The only thing left to do was the vacuuming. She was plugging the vacuum into the socket when her mother appeared in the doorway and stopped as if she had hit a wall.

"What happened in here?"

Jennifer tried to act as if she did this every Saturday. "Oh, nothing."

"Nothing? It's beautiful!" Their eyes traveled around the room.

Jennifer squirmed. "I just thought I'd clean up a little today."

"A little? It looks like Mary Poppins went through here saying, 'Clean, clean washing machine.' I don't think it's ever looked like this before."

Jennifer tried to smile but guilt was washing over her and it was hard. She managed a weak one as they surveyed the room. Maybe she had overdone it. She felt her mother looking at her. "Jennifer, is something wrong?"

"No, what could be wrong?"

"I'm not sure. But you're not acting like yourself."

Jennifer felt panic setting in. It made her sound angry. "You don't trust me."

"What?"

"Here I do all this . . . and all you can say is, 'Is something wrong?' Why does there have to be something wrong? Why can't I just want to help you out?"

"Jennifer, don't you think you're overreacting? All

I said was, 'Is something wrong?' I didn't attack you."

There was an uncomfortable pause.

"It was going to be a surprise," she said. She felt awful.

Again there was that uncomfortable pause. Then her mother smiled. "I'm sorry, Jen. It's just that it was such a surprise. I think it's great that you want to help me out a little." Jennifer felt a deep rush of relief spread through her.

"It's all right, Mom," she said. All she wanted now was to get out of this conversation. But her mother turned to look at the room one more time. "Jen, I just want to know, if there's anything bothering you" — she stressed the word "anything" — "will you promise to let me in on it?"

"I'm fine, Mom. Really."

"OK." Her mother suddenly grinned and kissed the top of her daughter's head. "Well, you did a great job in here and I'm proud of you. Oh, I almost forgot the reason I came in in the first place. Your invitation to the dance came, and Angela wants you to meet her at The Rink early today. You girls sure are practicing a lot. You must be getting good." She was halfway down the hall. She didn't notice that Jennifer had gone into shock.

# 11

# The Jennifer Jump

"Dance?" Jennifer said again. "How can I go to a dance?"

The two girls were at the rink again. For the fourth time in a week, working on wing control.

"I don't know. We'll figure something out. Now, just concentrate on the jump."

"You know, I'm working as hard at skating with wings as I did without them. Harder. I'm spending my whole vacation here."

Early every morning, when there was no one else on the ice and the men were too busy setting up to pay much attention to them, they rushed to The Rink. They headed straight for the bathroom, crammed themselves into the small space, and locked the door. The first time that Jennifer had emerged, wing covers attached and flowing, Reggie, who owned The Rink, had gaped disbelievingly. He had shook his head, desperately trying to suppress the chuckle that had burst out. Then, shaking with laughter, he had turned to answer the telephone.

Jennifer had wanted to die. She stared straight ahead, fastened her eyes on the bench across the room, and marched past him without saying a word, the great drapes flowing out from her back and dripping down toward the floor. When she sat down to put on her skates the gauze dripped over her face. She swiped at the wing covers and they floated out and back gently.

"They're too long," she had hissed at Angela.

"You're not going to skate with those things?" asked Don as he passed the girls on his way to the back room.

"Costume," muttered Angela.

"Don't trip," said Don.

"I feel like such a jerk," said Jennifer as they stepped out onto the ice and started round and round for their warm-up.

The chiffon wouldn't leave her alone. It kept floating in front of her face or catching over her arms. On the back crossovers it was impossible. But it was the spins that really did her in.

"It's hard enough without these things flapping at me," she complained as she slapped them away again. They came waving back and she took another swing at them. "I told you they were too big!" she turned accusingly.

"Well, I guess they are kinda long," admitted Angela. "Don't worry about it. We'll trim them tonight and they'll be perfect, believe me. Try a lunge."

"A lunge?" Jennifer looked doubtful. "Well . . ."

She took a long stride, then dipped. She felt the gauzy stuff catch under her skate and she landed hard.

"There's something wrong, Jen. You've got to keep them out of the way."

"Oh, smooth, Angela. Thanks a lot." Disgusted, Jennifer picked herself up off the ice and headed off the rink, tripping. Angela scrambled along behind, reaching out to gather up the chiffon like a train. "Not to worry. Jen, really. It'll be great once we get the kinks worked out. They just need a trim or something."

That night they trimmed the wing covers. And now they sort of floated wispily out a foot or so from the seams, little puffs of chiffon exuberantly pouring out behind her, catching the air as she skated. The wings were light against her legs, brushing her with each gliding movement. It was beginning to feel good, as if they were almost normal.

And she was beginning to use them. At first it was difficult to gauge the lift and the amount of wing movement she needed — too little and she scooted across the ice, her wings flapping and her feet out of sync, too much and she felt as if she'd be out of control. She practiced spinning with her wings tight against her, opening them slightly to slow her down, then closing them again to speed up.

She was afraid to open them too much; she could just see herself spinning like a corkscrew into the ceiling and surprising the people upstairs. Or crashing through the windows at the far end of the rink and soaring out into the little enclave of gardens behind the brownstones. She could just see herself making a U-turn over the bronze horses or the goldfish pond, zooming up over roofs to Madison Avenue, then landing and opening the door to The Rink and walking calmly up the steps as if nothing had happened.

"What are you giggling at?"

"Nothing." And she took off with a powerful stroke. Just once she had told Angela about spinning up through the floor above and was afraid of the sudden gleam that had come into her eyes. Now she kept her fantasies to herself.

She loved coming in early in the mornings. When school was open she never did and when she came in to practice it was always crowded. The ice was always chipped where the jumpers had dug in with their toe picks, and it was ragged and bumpy. But now it was beautiful. It had been sprayed the night before and had hardened evenly; there were no ruts, not even a blade scratch on it. Only Reggie's sneakers had left strange, flat footprints over the glistening surface.

When they glided out onto it they could hear their blades whispering, cutting so slightly into the smooth white surface. Behind them, their skates left flowing lines, light and clear on the ice. Round and round they went and then trails, like silken threads, cut into the ice and began to intertwine and cross, like spun cotton candy. And when they left the edges of the rink to go into the center, one flowing string broke off from the web and followed them.

Jennifer thought it was beautiful.

As Angela stood lookout, Jennifer began to practice her routine. "On the wings of a snow white dove," she sang quietly. "He sends His" — and a series of three turns sent her waltzing — "own sweet love." She could feel the music inside of her. She didn't have to think of which steps to do anymore, but only of the way she executed them and how she felt when she did them. She prepared for a spiral, bent her knees, straightened, and went into her arabesque. She felt her leg reaching out behind her, her arms stretching backward, her head up, her wings opening just slightly. A thin wave of cool air swept under them. She bent her body down as far as she could, and then suddenly there was a new pressure under her wings. They opened midarabesque and up she went!

"Whhooaa!" her voice rose. She was still in the pose, sailing above the ground. "Whhooa!" She tilted. She reached for the ground with her skating leg, but there was nothing there. Her arms began to paw at the air, circling as if she were treading water, flapping frantically as she tried to land. Her feet were scrabbling for a foothold. She tried to press her wings down. The windows were coming up fast — too fast! They were nearly on top of her! She banked to the left, ducked her head, and her inside edge caught the ice just in time. She swung in again toward the center, then plunged to the ice. She slid ten or twelve feet on her stomach, then came to a stop.

Angela was racing toward her. "It's a new jump! You invented a new jump!"

Jennifer couldn't even move.

"It's a new jump! There's never been a jump like it! I can't believe it!" Angela was almost jumping up and down.

Jennifer lay back on the ice waiting for her heart to stop the pounding rat-a-tat in her chest. Little screaming waves were coursing through her body. Angela didn't seem to notice.

"Come on! Try it again!" She reached down, grasped one arm, and pulled. "Come on, Jen, up! Try it again. What did you do? It was fabulous!" There was no answer from the ice. "Jen?" Jennifer opened her eyes and stared up at her. "Jen?" Still no answer, just a frantic panting as Jennifer tried to catch her breath. "Are you all right?"

She nodded.

Angela jumped back into action. "Well, don't scare me like that. Come on," she said as she yanked at her, "try it again."

"Will you quit it!" Jennifer managed, slapping at her. "Wait a minute, will ya!" She sat up and rubbed her thigh where she had hit the ice on that long slide. When she finally looked up again, she said, "What did I do?"

"It was a . . . I don't know, a . . . float."

"A what?"

"I don't know. You started with a spiral and then your wings went up. Then you went up. Come on." Angela grabbed her again and Jennifer struggled to her feet. "No one else will be able to do it. They'll name it after you."

"What are you talking about?"

"Your jump!" Angela was getting impatient. "Don't you get it? You invented a jump!"

Jennifer was brushing the clumped snow off her jeans.

"You know how they name things after people? The Salk Vaccine? The . . . the Kurt Thomas Flair? This'll be the Jennifer Jump!" She grabbed her arm. "Imagine having something named after you. And," her voice rose in stunned and sudden triumph, "I'll bet you could even beat Penelope at freestyle with that!"

"Oh, come on . . ."

"She couldn't top it! When the judge saw it, he'd flip! He'd have to give it to you!"

Jennifer pushed her away and backed up, staring at her. Angela's eyes were shining with excitement.

"I don't even know what I did."

"I told you. It was a spiral that went up. It's easy."

Jennifer backed away, silent.

"Just imagine," — there was a wheedling tone in Angela's voice — "all those people watching you. And, after your impossibly high jumps that no one else can match, and your spins, then, suddenly, you do something that no one else has ever done. It's . . . the . . . Jennifer Jump!

"They realize what they've seen. The crowd gasps with surprise. They're stunned, watching you skate as no one has ever skated before. And then . . ."

"You've read too many Wonder Woman comic books."

"Oh, shut up! Believe me, all you need is a little practice."

In her mind Jennifer could see it: the spins that could be slowed and quickened by a twitch of a wing; the high leaps and the flowing grace with which she could land them. And then — the Jennifer Jump!

She could feel the way her body would feel, hear the stunned cheers as they broke from the audience. The wonder and amazement on her friends' faces, the astonished pride in her mother's eyes. Her father would fly up just for the test. She would lift her shining face to the crowds as they poured onto the rink, their arms outstretched. It would be just as she had dreamed it as she lay awake at night looking at the full moon . . . the moon like a skating rink . . . with her dancing over its surface. And beyond the crowd, Penelope watching her in awe. And Samantha, as jealous as hell.

She could see it all.

"What did I do?" she asked.

The first day Jennifer hit the wall eight times. She went home aching. Somehow, what she had done by accident was impossible when she tried to do it on purpose.

"Come on!" Angela was always there, egging her on. "Try it again. You know that wall is there. Why don't you count faster? Up, two three . . . down, two three."

Or, when she had begun to get the hang of it, "You're landing on the wrong foot, dodo! Anybody can do that! It's the foot you went up on you land on."

Or, "Come on, Jen, it's got to look more natural. Just get the wings up and then down, fast. You're up there too long. It looks like a float instead of a jump. You can't be so obvious!"

Jennifer sat on the ice again, rubbing her leg.

"Well, you try it! You know, Angela, I'm putting in all the work and you just stand there jabbering at me!"

"Well, that's what a coach does."

"Well, I'm getting sick of it. Why don't you work on your own routine for a change." As she struggled to her feet a new shower of snow fell from her jogging pants.

"Well, first of all, I am. And second, you're the one with the wings, not me. And you're the one who wants to win. I'm just trying to help! You know what the trouble is?"

"What trouble?"

"Your trouble. You don't have enough room to practice. One false move and you hit the wall. One of these days you'll fly out the windows." Jennifer looked up quickly. "You need more room to practice."

Jennifer felt very quiet inside suddenly. Her voice sounded very low and very suspicious. "Now what?"

"You've outgrown this place." Then she said it again. "I think you ought to fly."

# 12

# *Flying*

"Fly? Are you on that again?"

"But don't you even want to fly?"

"I guess so. But this is New York, remember? Where do you think I can go without thousands of people seeing me?" Her skates were swinging over her shoulder, her wings brushing against her legs in an easy, gentle motion.

The two girls were walking through Central Park. The trees were turning a faint, whispery apple green and the sky was a very deep blue. And no matter which way they turned, there were people — people roller-skating and people walking, people jogging, biking, dog walking, kiting on Sheep's Meadow.

"Wow! Look at that one!" A kite, fifteen feet long, looking like a rainbow, danced across the sky. Jennifer shaded her eyes and watched it spiraling and shimmering as it twirled. A long tail ribboned out, flickering in the sun.

Angela stopped on the path. "Jen . . ."

"What?"

"Do you remember the hang glider kite we saw? It was like a giant balloon." Her voice was slow, as if she were thinking aloud and trying to figure something out.

"Well, I'm not sure."

"Oh, you remember. We were walking over by the Met. Your mom saw it first, remember? It was life-size. We all thought it was a man up there." Her voice was rising, building with excitement. "Remember? Think! Everyone was pointing. It came out from over the trees and . . . Come on, Jen, you were as excited as everyone else. You thought he was going to crash."

"Oh, yeah . . ."

"It was a kite!"

"Yeah?" Jennifer's voice was slow and suspicious. "So?"

"Well, I have lots of string."

"No."

"All we have to do is tie it on and everyone would think you were a kite."

"No!"

"Why not? You'd find out if you could really fly! You'd be up there!" She pointed toward the streaming, spiraling rainbow, its tail floating out across the cloudless sky. "Can't you even think what it would feel like?"

"NO!"

They walked along in silence. Angela looked mad. "I don't see why you won't do it."

"You act as if I'm spoiling your fun. First of all, I don't know if I can really fly. And I don't want to get killed, OK?"

"OK."

Jennifer kicked at a bottle cap on the path. "Besides," she paused, "people would be around to see me take off."

Angela spun around to face her. "Not if we do it right. All we have to do is find one little isolated spot, really early. And once you're even ten feet off the ground no one would dream you were real. I mean, people just don't think that way."

"But you just said . . ."

"Besides, I'd have this string on you. I've got a whole long roll of it from that plastic kite Dad got me at the beach. It's not even tangled or anything."

"Yeah. You never even got it off the ground."

"And if you really can't do it you'll never get off the ground."

"I don't know, Angela." Jennifer suddenly had a vision of herself up there, spiraling with the kite, float-ing in that immaculate, blue, immense space. She held her breath. She could almost feel herself weightless, free.

"I know what I'm talking about," Angela rattled on. "You'll be fine. Look, it's logical. If you can fly at the rink you can fly in the sky, right?"

"You really think so?" The sky was getting bluer.

"I'm your best friend, right? If I weren't so sure I'd say so."

"Well, I'll think about it."

"You will? Wow!"

Early the next morning the sky was blue again and the wind ruffled along, a perfect little breeze. The two girls were walking toward Sheep's Meadow. It was a huge expanse with a few clumps of trees here and there. A gray cement footpath ran around it and then, beyond, man-made forests with walks, rinks, ponds, and playgrounds were tucked in here and there. Sheep's Meadow was the one place where Jennifer could feel space, real space, opening up like a dome and widening out around her, forever.

But she wasn't thinking about that now. She was feeling her heartbeat. With each step, each slap of the wings against her legs, her heart jumped too. "Oh, Ange, I'm scared. What if . . ."

"There's nothing to be nervous about. Look," she said as she opened her PBS tote bag, "we've got plenty of string." The shiny nylon string was wound around a plastic tube shaped like a rolling pin, with bright red wings on either side.

"It doesn't look like very much."

"No problem. It goes on for miles and miles. Now, what we'll do is tie it around your wrist and that way you can signal me if you have to. I've got it all figured out. One tug means you're headed for the trees. Two tugs means that you should turn right, and three even tugs means you have to turn left. Two short tugs, like this, de-dum, means that people are coming, and . . ."

Panic was rising. "I'll never remember all of this."

"That's why I wrote it all down." She pulled a piece of paper out of her pocket and unfolded it. "See. Just put it in your pocket and if you get confused, you can take it out and read it." She sounded triumphant. Jennifer was looking over the list of directions. It looked like a long one. She closed one eye and looked at Angela cockeyed.

"Up there?"

"Sure. What difference does it make where you are? You can still read, can't you?"

"Oh, Lord." Jennifer groaned as she stuffed it into her pocket.

"Hey, this looks like a great spot." Spread out before them was the great lawn of Sheep's Meadow.

Jennifer took a deep breath as she looked out over it. There was only one other person there; another kiter, the one with the spiral kite of the day before. It was already unraveling against the sky, way across on the other side of the field.

"OK." Angela put down the tote bag and sat down on the grass. "Here, you need some strength. I brought apples and some juice" — she was emptying her bag on the lawn — "the string, a camera . . ."

"Don't you dare!"

"OK, OK, don't be so touchy. Oh, yes, sunglasses. It might be really glary up there. Knee pads from skating. I guess that's it." She cheerfully bit into an apple. "Don't you want one?"

"I'm too nervous."

"Don't worry. It'll be fine. I know . . ."

"If you say 'I know what I'm talking about' one more time, I'm leaving."

"Sorry." Angela turned to the field. "See, it looks good. I told you there wouldn't be anyone here."

"What about him?" Jennifer nodded toward the man on the other side of the Meadow. He was running along, his head tilted back, watching his kite.

Angela barely looked up. "Not to worry. He's too far away to notice anything. Besides, he's not paying any attention. Now, let's see . . . how's Dawn?"

Jennifer glanced back. "They're OK." She fluttered them for a moment, just to test them out. They were still there. "Oh, God, I'm scared." Her heart was thumping against her rib cage. "I can't believe I'm doing this."

"Now, just put out your hand and I'll tie on the

string." She leaned over Jennifer's outstretched arm. "I think it ought to go around twice, just to make sure. Oh, Jen, I'm so excited! I can't stand it! How do you feel?"

"You're not listening to me, Angela." Then she sighed. "I don't know. I really do wonder what it's like up there; if it's like flying in a plane or swimming or something." She felt her heart lurch again. "Scared," she said. "Really scared. And if my mother ever finds out . . ."

"OK. Now." Angela really didn't seem to hear her. She was too involved with the string. "Is it tight enough?"

"I guess so."

"Now, I don't want to make a bow. It might come undone . . . there, that's better." Jennifer looked down. The string was tied tightly in a series of little knots like her mother put on packages. She was attached. And Angela was unraveling the rolling pin. "Now, how do we do this?"

"What?"

"I'll keep hold of the string and you start running."

"It's supposed to be the other way around," said Jennifer. "A kite can't run."

"But you're not a normal kite. Now, if you run against the wind, and put Dawn out little by little, you ought to go up easy." She wet her finger and put it out to test the wind. "It's coming from up there," she said. "Perfect."

Jennifer stared up at the sky. The spiral kite was tumbling, then drifting in the air, its rainbow colors dancing in space. In a few minutes she'd be up there, too. She couldn't believe it. A surge of excitement filled her. She wanted to be up there. She really did.

"Jennifer!" She jumped. "Look, you've got to pay attention. You ought to test them out first. Just a little flutter to make sure you can really get off the ground."

"Is anyone watching?"

Angela looked around slowly, then shook her head. "No." There was no one in sight.

Jennifer nodded solemnly. She stood up as straight as she could and unfurled her wings. She let them out against the air. It felt wonderful with the cool air running under Dawn instead of their being cramped up against her back. For a moment she just let the delicious breeze play against them, running off behind and into space.

Angela's voice brought her back again. "Jen, are you fluttering? Nothing's happening."

"Not yet. You're sure no one's there?"

"Positive."

Jennifer hesitated, holding back.

"Come on, Jen, we don't have that much time. It's a quarter of eight already. The Jog-a-Thon starts at nine."

"Ohmagod, I forgot that."

"Don't worry about it. Just get started, OK?"

"OK. Here goes." She looked at Angela one more time. "Wish me luck." Her throat felt dry. Her breath was shallow and gasping.

Angela gulped. "Good luck."

"This is it." She felt herself stalling.

"Yep."

"OK. Here goes." She stood in the vast, empty field. Her eyes followed the string floating out from her wrist, attached, at the other end, to the bobbin in Angela's hands. She took one last deep breath, then wiggled her shoulders just a little. Behind her she could feel the breeze caught then released from her trembling wings. Her feet lifted from the ground, then touched down again. It was working. She opened her wings to a half span.

There was a surge she had never felt before, a thrilling, open release as she fanned her wings out behind her and felt the wind rushing up beneath them, lifting her up. She felt the string pull taut.

"Run!" she shouted.

Angela took off. At the end of the string she could feel Jennifer's weight rising, tugging for more and more string to be let out. The holder whirled in her hands.

Jennifer was climbing, whirling like the ballerina on her music box, round and round, higher and higher. Angela was the center of an invisible whirlpool, getting smaller and smaller, way down below. Branches with their tiny traces of buds passed by, and then the uneven brush of the treetops. And she was still going up. Over and beyond the trees, the hazy, gray city of skyscrapers was circling. And then, the sky.

Down below, Angela was motionless. Jennifer lifted her arm to wave and tilted. Her heart plummeted. She heard a long, faint scream and righted herself. She had never thought about steering. She'd have to do some experimenting.

She put both arms out to the side and they seemed to balance her. She lowered one arm slightly and her body tilted; both arms over her head and she lay horizontally. She tilted to the right. She turned, straightened out, and tilted to the left. She raised a shoulder and her whole body swerved again. She S-curved through the sky and did a figure eight. A new current swept under her body and she tipped and swooped with it. The wind changed and her wings automatically began to pump to hold her afloat. It was like dancing. She felt like singing. Up and up she went, then over and down.

She discovered subtle twists and movements of her body, changed her speed and direction, learned to listen to the wind. Her wings spread out behind her, opened fully, then snapped shut, and she twisted like a corkscrew; she swept them open again and she soared. Jennifer looked down. All of Central Park was budding and a thin veil of green hung over the trees. Here and there the park was splashed with brilliant streaks of yellow flowers and sprinkled with pink and white clouds of blossoming trees.

Above her space went on forever and she was a part of it; part of the air, of the power of the sky, held by the currents yet free. Tentatively she raised one leg in a flying variation of the Jennifer Jump and began to sing: "On the wings of a snow white dove." She laughed and the laughter rippled out around her. She really was the dove, as she started her freestyle routine. She turned and flowed into it, skating in the sky. "He sends His perfect . . ." She swirled and twirled.

There was a tug on her wrist. She stopped midair, slowed, and peered down. She could hardly see Angela anymore. She was just a tiny dot in the field. To her right another dot was traveling quickly. Another tug pulled at her wrist. She remembered the list in her pocket. She crossed her arm over her body to get at it. She twisted and plummeted.

Sky and trees spun by as she dropped. She heard a

long scream. Instinctively her arm went out and she was righted. A stream carried her upward again and she let herself be carried. Her whole body pounded and trembled, she could hear her breath wheezing and gasping. She had dropped so quickly! She steadied herself and felt her heartbeat slow.

Ohmagod, they'd put the list in the pocket she couldn't reach.

Suddenly she was aware of where she was. All that sky! And she was so tiny in it, hanging in it . . . alone . . . up there. All alone. Everything was so still; only her wings, swinging up and down, moved.

Another tug pulled her back. One tug. What did that mean? She'd have to get into her pocket. She took a deep, shivering breath and kept her wings moving. She'd have to use the hand with the string attached. With a quick motion she thrust her hand into her jeans pocket and then out again. Nothing.

She waited for a moment, gliding, preparing herself, then poised to try it again. Her wings whipped back and forth behind her. "One, two." She thrust more quickly. The tips of her fingers caught the paper and drew it out. Three frantic tugs jerked her arm like the strings would a marionette. Her fingers opened. The paper flew out into space. She made a grab for it, but the breeze had already taken it. She dove awkwardly and timidly, no longer sure of what to do. It fluttered, twirling, out of her reach, turning silver then dark as the sun caught it.

Desperately she leaned over and looked down. On the field the dot seemed to be jumping up and down. Angela was dancing wildly, waving her arms and pulling on the string like a bell ringer. Jennifer's arm was cranked up and down like a puppet's. She fluttered frantically, trying to hold herself upright, peering down. What did Angela want?

Then Jennifer saw it: the other kite. Its spirals were turning, churning in the wind. Its tail was floating out gracefully behind. It was coming toward her.

She tried to dive, then caught herself. Somehow she had gotten too close to the trees and her line was caught. The kite was still coming. She had to get away. She plucked at the knot they'd tied on her wrist. It was too tight! She flapped desperately, trying to keep steady. And the spiraling kite chugged methodically toward her.

She started to struggle, feeling as if she were doing some strange, uncontrollable dance up there in the middle of nothing. The kite made its way evenly, calmly, toward her. She tugged on the string, pulling, trying to break it. It wouldn't budge. Her sunglasses tipped off an ear and dangled for a second before they fell off altogether, and the sun's full glare hit her full force. She blinked against it. And as her arm went up to shield her eyes she lost her bearings and dropped. She struggled to open her wings.

Something hit her kite string.

The impact sent her swaying wildly back and forth like a pendulum. When she finally slowed enough to look down, she saw the kite. Her string was caught, wrapped around it. It was struggling in the wind to free itself, opening and closing like an accordion. She was losing control, her wings flapping in one direction, the string pulling in the other, the thing getting more and more tangled.

There was a ripping sound as something beneath

her went limp. As she watched, the bright colors of the kite tore apart. Pieces of it went sailing down through the sky. The string snapped. The whole, mangled contraption fell hurtling toward the earth while she spun in confusion toward the trees.

She reached out for the branches.

# 13

## Disaster, Total Disaster!

"Jennifer! Jennifer!"

She opened her eyes. Angela was racing toward her, tears streaming down her horrified face. "Jen . . . talk to me. Are you all right? Oh, Jen!"

She was clinging desperately to a branch in a tree, heaving, scrabbling for a foothold. Dawn vibrated in the twigs above.

She closed her eyes and managed a nod. "I can't move," she said. She was trembling uncontrollably.

"Are you hurt? Oh, Jen!"

"No . . . I . . . I . . ."

"Jen, you've got to get down. He's coming!'

"I can't."

"The man with the kite is really mad! He . . ."

"I can't." She felt totally and horribly helpless. She held on tighter.

"But . . ."

From around the bend a furious man charged toward them, dragging the remains of his mangled kite.

"What do you think you're doing!" he screamed at Angela. "Look at this! Look at this! It's ruined! This kite cost me a hundred and fifty bucks and look at it!"

He stopped midscream and stared up at Jennifer, lopsided and clinging in a crook of the tree, her eyes tightly shut.

"Where's the rest of my kite?" he screamed at her.

She cringed and pointed to the ground behind the tree where the tangled mess of string and torn rainbow lay in a heap.

"Look at it! Just look at . . ." He stopped and gaped. "Where the hell did you come from?"

Angela looked at her feet. Jennifer shook her head. She looked at his ruined kite and felt a sob rising. It had been so beautiful floating up there. She whimpered and tried to swallow.

"I . . . I'm sorry."

"How did you get up there?"

"She flew." Angela turned her face up toward Jennifer. "Come on, let's get out of here."

"I can't." She shifted slightly, gulped back a sob, and looked guardedly at the man staring up at her. "I think Dawn is . . . is caught."

"Ohmagod, how did that happen?"

"I don't know. Just get me out of here."

"OK." Angela reached up for a branch and swung up on it. "I'm coming up." She heaved herself up into the tree. The man gaped as she straddled the bough and looked out over the field. "Wow," she said, "what a view."

Jennifer clutched at her. "I'm stuck." They looked up at the branches wobbling above them.

"Try wiggling free."

"I am." She twitched her shoulders. "It hurts." She looked toward the man down below. "I wanna die."

"OK. Let me try." She edged closer, balancing herself. The bough above seemed to be bending low, as if caught. Jennifer shifted slightly and the twigs bowed with the movement.

Angela snapped off a dead twig and swiped at the bough. It bounced. Jennifer could feel her wing bobbing up and down buoyantly. "Stop that!"

"I was just trying to get it loose."

"Well, it isn't working. Try something else."

"OW! Be careful!"

"I am."

"What are they doing, Mommy?" Through the branches Jennifer could see a woman and child strolling toward them.

"I don't know, sweetheart. Maybe this man knows. What's going on?"

Oh, no, they'd stopped to chat. She clenched her fists. All three heads tilted up at her.

"How do I know? All I know is that they ruined my kite." The man snatched it up and shook it. "Look at it! A hundred and fifty bucks shot to hell."

The little boy tugged at his mother's skirt. "Mommy . . ."

"What are you doing up there?" The woman called up. "Are you all right?"

"Oh, God." Jennifer tried to shrink back against the tree. "I'm a sideshow, Angela. Do something."

Angela crept her way down the limb toward her again.

"But they're down there."

"Forget them. The thing is . . . I can't see anything. I'll hold you and you see if you can pull it free." Jennifer took a deep breath, looked up, and nodded. Angela wrapped her arm around her. Jennifer reached up slowly toward the tip of her wing. She tilted her head back to see better. And lurched. Angela swung out, then in again. Jennifer felt the bark scrape against her leg. There was a gasp from down below.

"Christ, they're gonna kill themselves! What the hell are you two doing?"

Jennifer was hanging crooked, swinging slightly. Her free wing was half opened and the other still stuck and quivering. The whole bough above her was shaking.

Angela was hauling herself back up onto the branch.

"OK. That's it! I'm getting a cop. You kids are crazy." He swiped his ruined kite from the ground and strode off, dragging it behind him, jerking it over the ground. At the edge of the path he swooped it up and shoved it violently into a garbage can. They could hear him ranting. "A hundred and fifty bucks down the tubes! And they're trying to kill themselves." He turned the bend in the road, and the voice faded into the distance.

Jennifer's heartbeat was wild. She twisted violently and was jerked back, flat against the tree.

"Mommy, what are they playing? Can I try?"

"JEFFREY!" The sharpness in her voice brought Angela to life. Jeffrey was at the foot of the tree, his arms wrapped around the trunk, one leg lifted, looking for a foothold on it.

"We're going, Jeffrey," the mother said as she grabbed him by the arm and pulled him toward the path. His voice sirened back up to them. "But I wanna see . . ."

"No, we're going to find someone to help them. They must be stuck. Come ON, Jeffrey!"

"I don't wanna. I wanna see."

Their voices, too, grew fainter and for the first time the girls were alone. Off in the distance a few joggers in school colors trotted up the path toward the starting line. They curved onto the path running under the tree. "Can you see? Are they ours?" whispered Jennifer. Angela shook her head. "No, that's Brearly," she glanced at her watch. "Now, we've really got to get out of here. Maybe I could just pull it free."

"Pull what!"

Angela reached up, hunting blindly for the wing, found the edge, and pulled. The branch bent low. Jennifer could feel the wing stretching. It was going to tear! "Let go!" she screamed. The branch snapped up. She bounced with it once or twice then toppled sideways. Angela shot to one side.

"What are you doing!" she screamed at Jennifer.

"It was going to tear! I could feel it!"

"You almost killed me!"

"It . . . it hurts!" Jennifer was about to break into tears.

Jennifer twisted again. But it was no good. And her foot was falling asleep. "Oh, great." She leaned back heavily and slumped. She felt her lips trembling. "I can't move, Angela. What am I going to do?"

Angela concentrated on some blood oozing out of a scratch on her leg. She licked it off her finger. "Sshhh . . . I'm thinking."

On the other side of the field a family was settling on the grass. More joggers were strolling across the lawn. Soon the park would be full. It was all over.

She was trapped forever. Angela would have to leave sometime and she would have to stay there. Angela would have to bring her food. And her homework. In the winter she'd need a buffalo robe to keep her warm. Maybe her mother would bring her flowered comforter. People would come from miles around to stare at her. From all over the world. Angela would probably charge admission.

They'd decorate her for Christmas.

Or the doctor would bring his scalpels and stuff with him and he'd have to stand in the tree to operate. They'd haul huge mirrors up the tree so he could see what he was doing. "Mirrors . . . ," she murmured. Then she suddenly came to life. "Angela . . . mirrors!"

"Mirrors!" shouted Angela, already scrambling down the tree. "You stay here."

"Where do you think I'm going?"

Jennifer wiggled her toes and sent a tingling pain coursing up from her spongy foot and into her leg. It was excruciating, but she tried to put some weight on it. You were supposed to stomp on your foot when it went to sleep. Oh, God. Tears were spilling down her face. What would her mother say?

She could just see the headline: GIRL LIVES IN TREE. She pulled back a sob, stretched out, and peered down through the branches. She could just make out Angela fumbling with her PBS bag at the base of the tree.

"There's a mirror in here somewhere. I know I put one in when I . . ." She could hear Angela mumbling as she turned the bag upside down and dumped its contents on the grass. Then a cry of triumph: "I knew it!"

"Hurry!"

"Now," Angela panted as she scrambled up again, "the thing is, if I can see Dawn it'll be easy." She pulled the bough down as far as possible and aimed the mirror toward the shaking twigs above.

"Aha!" Jennifer could feel the touch on her wing. She held herself very still.

"Found it! There's a twig caught all right; one here . . . and here . . . and it's twisted here." As she spoke Jennifer felt a series of gentle tugs and manipulations on her wing. She held her breath. Then it sprang suddenly free. She sagged as her legs collapsed and she sank to the crook of the tree.

"Are you all right?" Angela had made her way down again and was bent over her.

Jennifer nodded. "My leg's asleep." She tried to massage it and a surge of pins and needles made her catch her breath. "Just tell me one thing," she whispered. "Is it torn?"

"No." Angela was examining the spot carefully. "Just a little bent. Maybe we could iron it."

"NO!" screamed Jennifer. "Don't you dare touch it!"

"OK, OK, I won't do a thing." They jumped at a loud bang in the distance. "Ohmagod, the race! Come on, let's get out of here." Angela leaped to the ground. Jennifer shifted gingerly and put her weight on her foot. A searing tingle pierced her leg. She groaned as she made her way down, sitting on one branch and sliding down to the next. The ground looked very far away. She sat on the lowest limb, edging herself off, held her breath, and pushed.

"Are you OK?"

Her tingling foot collapsed under her, and she sat

in a crumpled heap on the ground. The front line of runners was already coming into sight, pushing steadily forward down the curving path toward them. "My leg's asleep," she winced. "Oh, God . . . what a disaster." She shook her head and pounded her leg with her fist. "What a mess." A few joggers puffed past them on the walk.

Angela had started picking up her things and dumping them back into the tote bag. "Anyway, it turned out all right, didn't it?" She grabbed her friend's arm with sudden excitement. "And you flew, you really flew!"

On the walk more kids jogged by, eyes ahead, arms jerking, feet churning. "Come on," Angela said, "let's go. We've got to get out of here before someone we know shows up." She was jogging lightly in place.

Jennifer punched her foot and the tingles flew up her ankle and into her leg. "I told you. My leg's asleep."

"Well, pound it."

"What do you think I'm doing?" She struggled to stand and her ankle turned in under her.

"Stomp on it. Here, lean on me." The runners were a flood now, body to body, jamming the walk. Jennifer leaned heavily on Angela, trying to stamp while the tingles soared.

"Uh-oh." Angela was staring over Jennifer's head. "Look."

On the other side of the lawn the man with the kite was unmistakable. He was stomping toward them, gesticulating wildly toward their tree. A policeman was hurrying in his wake. Jennifer felt Angela grab her and drag her into the race. She stumbled in among the runners. Her leg was burning with pins and needles.

Her shoulder blades were aching and Dawn was flopping uncontrollably. Someone bumped her from behind and she stumbled, her ankle a rubbery, uncontrollable thing. She kept her eyes on the bobbing heads in front of her and concentrated on moving her legs. It was agony.

She lurched to one side. "Hey . . . watch it!" She pitched into someone else. "Hey, what the . . . Jennifer!"

Samantha. Oh, NO!

The whole gang was there, running as a pack.

Samantha's curls bounced as she paced next to her. "Look who's here, the athlete." Jennifer tried to smile, but her breath was coming in great, heaving gasps. Samantha jogged lightly by. "See you at the finish line." David grinned at her as he passed. Stacey passed, and Kathy and Heather and Peter; off they went, bouncing into the mass of bobbing heads.

Jennifer slowed. "I can't," she panted. "I can't." And she gave up. She limped to a standstill on the sidelines as the race poured by. The man with the policeman was nowhere in sight. She let Angela put her arm around her waist and lead her off.

"Disaster," she said. "Total disaster." She shook her head slowly, and subdued, they started across the meadow toward the edge of the park.

In the middle of the field a little boy was reeling his kite into the sky. Jennifer stopped and stared up at it; it looked so unfettered as it turned and twisted against a few puffy clouds. The people sprawled out over the lawn watched it lazily as it rolled along. Not one of them could know what it was like up there. But she did. She caught her breath; she could hardly breathe.

She felt Angela watching her.

"Jennifer?" Angela's voice was soft, as if afraid to break a spell. "Jen? What was it like?"

She'd never be able to explain it. "I don't know." She hunted for the words. "It was wonderful till the kite hit — like swimming, only freer. Like . . ." She felt a stinging behind her eyes again. There was no way she could explain it. "It was wonderful."

"Oh, Lord." Angela began to giggle. "What a day! If you could have seen yourself up there in the sky with your legs wiggling and . . ."

"What?"

Angela caught sight of Jennifer's face; she was glowering, her bright eyes glinting behind the teary red. "I'm sorry, Jen. I shouldn't laugh, but really, if you could have seen . . ."

Jennifer clenched her teeth and stared straight ahead. Wiggling? Funny? Angela would never understand.

"I promised my mother I'd baby-sit, Jen, or I'd go home with you. I'm dying to hear what it was like. Want to come to my house?"

"No, thanks." The silence between them was awkward.

"Anyway, we're going to drop our stuff off at Stacey's before the dance, right? So I'll meet you there."

But Jennifer hardly heard her. How could Angela think it was funny? Jennifer suddenly seemed fascinated by a flock of daffodils sprinkled over a little hillside.

Angela looked at her sideways. "The tree wasn't my fault, you know," she said. "You're not mad, are you?" The daffodils past, a dog straining on a leash seemed to hold the same fascination. "Jennifer, I didn't do anything!"

"I know, Angela." She paused and looked at her squarely for the first time since they'd started home. "But just do me a favor, will you? Just don't ever tell me you know what you're talking about again."

Then wearily she turned and limped off toward home. Up in the sky the kites flew with the wind. Behind her her wings flopped monotonously against her legs.

Dance?

# 14

# On the Way to the Dance

Angela had called twice that afternoon, but Jennifer really didn't want to talk to her. She ached all over and just wanted to soak in the tub and think about flying. And try to figure out a way to get out of the dance. Everything was so confusing. But even soaking was hard. She was afraid to get her wings wet, so she scrunched around and let them hang off the sides. The tub was sort of cold on her back and she shivered, pulled a towel down off the rack, and wrapped it around her shoulders. But, of course, it sort of humped up in the back and let the cool air in on her spine. She shifted again, putting her wings up against the wall. She felt them crunch; it was better the first way. Behind the door she heard the muffled ring of the phone again and waited for her mother's voice. Angela again. She really didn't want to talk to her; she was her best friend, but right now Angela was too much.

Her mother's voice came through the door. "Are you going to talk to her now and straighten out whatever's bothering you? Or is this thing going to go on? I don't have all day for these phone calls. I have work to do!"

"OK, OK . . . I'm coming out. Tell her I'll call her back."

She almost tripped over Cleopatra as she bounded out of the bathroom. She threw on her robe, then flung herself down on the bed. Above her, on the bulletin board, the dance invitation seemed to glow. Jennifer clenched her fist and hit one of the daisies on her bed.

"Jennifer?" Her mother was standing in the doorway. "What is it, honey? Is something wrong?"

Jennifer turned over fast and sat up. She pointed up to the card. "Yuk," she said miserably.

" 'Yuk'? You loved the last one."

"No, I didn't! It was crummy." Jennifer shook her head.

"That's not what you said at the time. I think your choice of words was 'Wow!' And you've been talking about this dance for weeks."

"It was gross! And I don't want to go!" She heard her voice rising but she couldn't stop it from coming out that way. She looked down quickly, very conscious that her mother was staring at her. She squirmed and turned her back further toward the wall.

"Honey, we all have jitters at times." Her mother had that concerned look in her eyes again. "We just have to try to work through them. Once you get there you'll have a great time." But Jennifer was shaking her head before her mother was halfway through the sentence. She was intent on tracing a daisy with her finger. She felt sulky. She knew she sounded difficult

· 119 ·

and stubborn and her mother wouldn't understand. All she really wanted to do was curl up against her and tell her the whole stupid thing. It was so tempting to blurt it out, but somehow the secret had seemed to move deeper in a crevice inside of her and was stuck there. She just shook her head listlessly.

"Please, Jen, if there's something bothering you, I wish you'd tell me about it."

But Jennifer's finger followed a stem as if it were of extraordinary importance.

"Has this anything to do with Angela? Are you two having a fight?"

Jennifer wished she would stop. Why couldn't she leave her alone?

The phone rang. And this time Jennifer leaped for it as her mother turned to leave the room. It was Stacey again.

"When you come over don't forget to bring your sleeping bag."

She shook her head helplessly. "I . . . I can't." She'd never even go to a sleepover again! "I've got a sprained ankle," she said. "I have to go to the doctor tomorrow."

"Angela said you were fine . . . your foot was asleep."

"She doesn't know everything. I did it on the way home."

"Well, what about tomorrow? You gonna call that off, too?"

Oh, God. The groan was so loud inside her she could almost hear it. "I can't . . . I've got to skate."

"I thought you said you sprained your ankle!" And then the crash of the phone on the other end. Now Stacey was mad, too.

Then Angela called, again.

"I just can't go to Stacey's," Jennifer said.

"OK, OK. I guess I'll meet you at the usual place. But you'd better take an Ace bandage or something, just in case."

A thin drizzle had started by the time Jennifer had left the house. She thought briefly about going back for her raincoat, but she'd have to cut holes in it, and anyway, she didn't want to have to face her mother again. That had been a close call. She had wanted to walk her to the church where the dance was, but Jennifer had fought the idea. If she went she'd probably end up staying and being a chaperone.

"Nobody's parents are taking them. They'll think I'm a baby. Besides, I'm meeting Angela." Her mother had studied her face for a moment. A new anxiety attack had gripped Jennifer as it looked as if there was going to be a stalemate. Then her mother had sighed and given her a quick kiss.

"Oh, Jennifer, I guess you're growing up. But I want you to call me when you get there. Understand?" Jennifer had nodded thankfully.

Now she trudged reluctantly up Seventy-eighth Street toward Madison Avenue, her eyes focused, unseeing, on the gray, pebbled pavement, her wings slapping with weary regularity on the backs of her legs, her heart beating rapidly with fear, her mind a million miles away. She had never dreaded anything so much. There was no way out. Not unless she just disappeared.

Maybe that was it! Maybe she just wouldn't show up. She could wander around for a few hours till it was over and get back just in time for her mother to pick her up. That was the one thing she hadn't been able to pull off. "No way." Her mother's voice had been absolutely firm. "You're not coming home in the dark alone."

A pair of legs jutting out across the sidewalk broke her thoughts. She hopped to one side to avoid a bag lady sprawled out over the pavement, leaning against the building. Her little blue eyes glinted up at Jennifer behind the wrinkles of embedded dirt. Jennifer's heart thudded against her chest as she hurried across the street. Maybe wandering around wasn't such a hot idea. Besides, it was going to rain. Nuts.

The museums would be closed and she didn't have the money for a movie. And if her mother ever found out that she went to a movie by herself . . . she didn't even want to think about that! Anyway, she could hardly fit in a seat. Her feet automatically kept to their path.

Besides, if her name wasn't checked off the list at the dance they'd call home. And her mother would panic. She'd call the cops and . . . She groaned aloud. She was sunk.

Why don't they just fly away?

She could actually feel them lifting off her back and leaving her free, disappearing up into the sky and leaving her behind. The wings would lift, then synchronize as they rose, a bodiless bird that would get smaller and smaller until it flew away into nothingness.

They slapped ponderously at her legs as she plodded on.

Then a thought stopped her cold. What if they were here to stay? That would be a nightmare. It was one thing to have them for a while to play with, like tap shoes you could take off when you wanted, but if she had to have them forever! She could just see herself, an old lady, hobbling down the street, clutching at the sides of the buildings, a plastic shopping bag, instead of her skates, swinging from her arm. A little gust of wind blew up under her wings and she gave a little hop. She'd better pay attention.

Angela was waiting for her at the bridal shop, gazing up at a new dress in the window.

"Isn't it beautiful," she breathed as Jennifer trudged toward her. "Look at those yards of chiffon. Can't you just see yourself in it?" She was wearing her plaid jeans, purple-with-pink-flowered sweatshirt, and black high-top Reeboks. Her PBS umbrella swung from her arm as she did a slow turn like a waltz. "You'd just float."

Jennifer's eyes narrowed. "Don't mention that word to me."

"Sorry." She tore herself away from the dress and turned up the street. The church was just a few blocks away.

"Are you still upset? Everything turned out all right, didn't it?"

Jennifer was silent.

"Well, didn't it?" Angela was trotting alongside, insistent.

"The only thing that turned out all right was that I'm still alive . . . and I'm not so sure that's so great right now."

"But nobody saw you, so . . ."

"Nobody saw? Nobody saw? What do you call the kite man? And that kid with his mother? And the jogging thing, forgodsake!"

Angela shrugged and dismissed them. "Oh, them.

Well, I mean . . . up there." She thrust her umbrella toward the threatening gray sky. "Wow, looks like it's really gonna come down. Let's go!"

Jennifer watched her as she quickened her step. She had definite reservations about this.

"Ange, are you really sure I should go to this thing?"

"Sure. Why not?"

Jennifer scurried along now to keep up, her wings bobbing along behind.

"Guess! Dance? Wings? Flip, flap. Remember?"

"Oh, nobody's gonna notice. All those flashing lights and everything? It'll be fine, believe me."

"I just can't dance. If I can just stand around and . . ."

"What if David asks you? You just can't stand there like a jerk. Anyway, it's not like there's close dancing or anything. All you have to do is stand around and jiggle. You can do that, can't you?"

"Well, I . . ."

"Besides, Samantha and her gang are going to be there. You can't let them think you're a wimp, can you?"

Jennifer clutched her bag. The bandage was neatly rolled inside. She could always duck into the ladies' room and wrap her ankle if she had to.

"Angela . . ." A wet splash spattered on Jennifer's forehead. She glanced up. Overhead the drops were forming and sliding off the edges of the awnings. Angela fumbled with her umbrella. She pushed it open and it arched over them, a little cockeyed. The handle was slightly bent and one spine had broken off. It hung, swinging gently, like a windshield wiper. "Be careful with that thing!" said Jennifer.

"I am." She turned it toward the back. A little gust

of wind blew the heavying mist under the umbrella. Jennifer felt her wings rise slightly with it and she pushed them down almost unthinkingly. "Let's just get there."

An uneasy feeling was building. The church was in sight but somehow it looked very far away through the misting rain. A little cold wind was rising and an ominous string of fear pulled at her. She quickened her step and huddled closer to Angela. Another wisp of a breeze caught her wings and played under them for a moment before swooping out again.

Overhead the umbrella swung, and there was an odd tingling in her wings as the rain fell and hung there. Jennifer had a sinking feeling. There was a new disaster coming; she just knew it. The two girls crept along the buildings. At the corner they stood back against the florist shop waiting for the light to change, Jennifer pressing her wings closely against the glass.

"When it turns we make a run for it, right?"

Jennifer nodded. The traffic light was a watery blur in the distance. She glanced at the people on the street. They weren't paying any attention to her. They were too busy fighting with their own umbrellas.

The light turned a wavering yellow. The two girls edged out toward the curb.

"Ready . . ." Angela leaned into a racer's starting position. The umbrella wobbled overhead. Jennifer nodded, bending low, and clutched at her friend's arm. "Set . . ." The light turned green. "Go!"

They spurted out into the street. Overhead, the umbrella swayed. For a moment it cruised out like a sail then sailed back again. The wind sent a curtain of rain swashing against them. Jennifer pressed on, pushing her wings down, keeping her eyes on the far curb. The wind caught her up and, with a little "Oh," she gave an unexpected hop. Then it suddenly calmed.

"I . . . I can't believe this is happening."

"We're almost there." But even Angela's voice had a foreboding about it.

They were halfway across before it tore at them.

Jennifer felt the umbrella pull up and around as the wind was sucked into it, changed directions, and slammed them from behind. She gasped as it hit her full force and carried her with it. Dawn fought it, but lost and opened. She tilted. She could feel her feet lift.

"No!" She heard her cry in the wind. She couldn't go up, she just couldn't! She clung to Angela, pressing down with all her strength.

"Quit it!" She heard Angela's gasp as she zoomed off sideways. "You're pulling me up!"

"I can't help it!" She lurched by. "It's got me!"

The wind ceased for a moment and the umbrella plummeted. When it parachuted up again a sudden sting pierced her wing as if a needle had plunged into it. She was flung with the wind, held rigid in the spokes, penduluming back and forth as the umbrella took her.

"Don't let go!" Jennifer screamed as she scudded backward. She felt herself rise, staggered over the curb, and kept her feet moving. Her eyes were tightly shut against the stinging rain. Angela was screeching something at her but she couldn't make it out. Then wind and rain died and she was flung against something hard.

She opened her eyes. The girls were huddled in the doorway on the corner of the street. She couldn't stop gasping for breath. Her hair was whipped and plastered against her face and it strung into her mouth. There was a strange numbness in her wing. Angela was fumbling with the umbrella.

"Don't close it!" she screamed as Angela reached for the umbrella latch and she felt her wing bend. "It's caught! Get it free! Get it free!" She knew she was hysterical and screaming, but she couldn't help it.

"Hold still . . . Where?"

"At the top! Get it out! Get it out!"

She could feel Angela's hands shaking as she grappled with the wires, bending them, pulling them out, and releasing the wing. Then she carefully drew out the spoke that had speared her.

There was a searing pain as Dawn was torn free.

The wing collapsed and Jennifer sank back. She felt Angela leaning heavily against her, panting.

"Are you all right?" she whispered.

"That was awful. It was worse than the tree."

"That was the weirdest thing I ever saw. How did you do that?" That was Samantha. The two girls looked out. Filling the doorway, under a canopy of umbrellas, curious, astounded faces stared in at them. At the back of the group David was staring at them openmouthed.

"Are you all right?" he asked. But Jennifer just stood there staring back and dripping.

"What were you doing? What was that, Jennifer, a new dance?" Jennifer cringed at the sound of Samantha's voice. "Honestly, they are so weird."

The giggles stabbed at her as they huddled wordlessly in the doorway. And then, "Oh, come on, Samantha, leave them alone." And the faces disappeared as "Can you believe it!" drifted back to them through the darkening rain. David was the last to go. He hesitated, but when Jennifer didn't say anything, he, too, turned and walked after them. The fading giggles echoed back to them.

Jennifer closed her eyes.

"That," said Angela, "was the pits."

Jennifer could feel the drops sliding down the edges of her wings, splashing on the black marble tiles. A throbbing in her wing where the spoke had stabbed her was beginning to pierce the numbness.

"What does it look like back there?" She forced the words out.

Angela lifted a trembling hand. "I don't know. Kinda strange. There's all this water just sorta hanging in the air . . . here." She tapped at it weakly. Jennifer felt the drops bounce halfheartedly then land again. She cringed. "Does it hurt?"

Jennifer nodded.

Angela brushed at Dawn a little. "I guess we've got to get to a bathroom or something and towel you down. Maybe one of those hot air dryers."

"They saw." Jennifer's voice was heavy and dull. "They really saw."

"But" — but even Angela sounded weak — "they couldn't really know . . . I mean, what they saw. It was so quick." Her voice was full of wonder. "It was just so quick."

She looked down at her umbrella. The spokes were pulled out and bent or torn off at the ends. There was a long tear through the S of the PBS and the handle looked like an L. "I guess this is ruined," she said. She pushed one of the spokes into her finger. It left a tiny dent. "Well" — the umbrella landed in the corner with a dull splash — "we can't stay here forever."

Jennifer raised her eyes suspiciously. "You don't expect me to still go, do you?"

They peered out into the street. Kids were heading down the block; groups of them splashing along and laughing, heads down, fighting the rain. No one was paying any attention to Jennifer and Angela. It would be so easy to slip around the corner, make a run for it, and head toward home.

# The Dance

"Where were you guys? I thought you were going to the race. Do you believe this weather? I'm soaked."

Stacey and Miranda were standing in the doorway looking in on them.

"Couldn't make it."

"Like you can't make my party?" Stacey stepped in out of the rain and eyed Jennifer coldly. "How's your ankle?"

A new gust of wind whipped in behind Stacey and Miranda. Stacey grabbed Angela's arm.

"Come on, let's get out of here before we're all blown away," Stacey continued. "God, you're wet. Don't you guys have an umbrella?" And Angela was pulled out into the rain. And away.

Jennifer froze.

"Aren't you coming?" Miranda was waiting there, dripping. "What's the matter with you? I'm soaked."

Jennifer hovered in the doorway. It was happening again. She peered out into the street, then took a step backward. Miranda staggered as someone sideswiped her. "Oh, forgodsake, come ON!" She reached out for Jennifer and pulled.

Jennifer pressed Dawn flat against her back and could feel the wet shirt clinging to them as they lay sticking against it. The rain pounded on Miranda's pink umbrella, then cascaded off the spines, washing down over her wings. They wobbled dangerously. She pressed them in again and tried to remember to limp.

"So?"

"Huh?"

"I said, 'What did you do to get her so mad?' Whoops!" She skirted a puddle and they sloshed on behind a bunch of boys careening across the sidewalk. "You look awful, Jennifer. You'd better do something about your hair. Oh, hi, Danielle. Did you find your bracelet?"

The sidewalk was teeming with kids flocking toward the wrought-iron gates of the churchyard. The crowd overflowed into the street and down the sidewalks, squealing and pushing, then squeezing in through the gates. "Sarah!" squealed Miranda, "did you go to the basketball game last night? It was so GOOD! Do you believe we actually won!"

Jennifer turned to look for a way out, but Miranda had a good hold on her and the crowd was already crushing in behind. They shuffled toward the bottleneck at the gates, then squeezed through and stepped down into the tiny courtyard. Jennifer stared at the back in front of her and felt the eyes of the person behind her staring. She could just picture the thousands of water drops following her, wobbling midair. She shivered. It was just a matter of time. Any second now and she was dead meat. She could hear the screams.

Behind her someone pressed in and she felt Dawn squish. She tensed. This was it. It was coming. She knew it. Any second . . .

But there was no "LOOK, WINGS!"; not even a "Did you know there's something weird on you?" She took a deep, trembling breath and was led on. Miranda was still jabbering. "Oh, Penelope never comes to these things. She's always off practicing." They were all wedged in tightly and wetly against each other, inching toward the door. The umbrellas made a canopy overhead, the rain pounding at them with the drops slipping through here and there. Just ahead she could see the umbrellas closing two by two as the kids reached the doorway and disappeared inside. There was no escape. The umbrella hovered overhead for a moment or so longer, then, with a shower spraying out over the girls, Miranda closed the latch. They stepped over the threshold and the droning sound of the rain ceased.

A pulsing beat of rock took its place, filtering up from below under the excited clatter and chatter. They surged toward it and followed it down a wide, winding staircase. At the top Jennifer paused and scanned the wide steps. Angela was nowhere in sight.

"Let's GO!" And she was pushed on.

Jennifer fastened her eyes on the door at the bottom of the stairs. She was almost there. Then she pushed through the narrow doorway into the huge room beyond and sprinted toward the bathroom.

"Wait a minute, honey, you have to sign in." A hand touched her shoulder, then sprang back. "You're soaking wet. Don't you have an umbrella?"

"Broke," she muttered, edging toward the wall. "Have to go to the bathroom."

"Just sign in first." The chaperone was wiping her

hands together delicately. Jennifer glanced toward the sign-in table. The mob was swarming around it, ten deep. She shrank back.

"I'm sorry, honey, but those are the rules; just to make sure your name is on the list, you know. We don't want anyone we don't know coming in here, now, do we?"

Jennifer shook her head mutely and turned toward the table.

Now the dance was almost over.

She had spent the first half hour in the ladies' room. The face that had stared back at her in the mirror was a nightmare, all blotchy and scared-looking, hair matted to the side of her face and streaming down her neck, the apple green bow in her hair soggy and hanging sideways. Her shirt was drenched.

"Oh, God." She was almost afraid to see what Dawn looked like, but she stood up on tiptoe and twisted toward the mirror. They were waterlogged, plastered against her shirt. There was a tiny red puncture where her wing hurt and a pale streak of pink running down along the veins. She reached out for the paper towels. Maybe she could press some of the water out.

A few minutes later sodden paper towels were everywhere and all she had reached were the edges. There had to be a better way. She closed her eyes, prepared for pain, and forced the wings open. They sprang away, flapping, and sent a shower spattering across the walls, then dripped onto the floor.

YUK! She leaned against the sink and hung them out behind her, like a cormorant, she thought dismally. Just like some stupid bird.

Where was Angela?

She was digging into her purse for a comb when she heard voices. She leaped for a stall and slammed the door just in time. The sounds of rock blasted loudly then grew faint again as the door closed.

"God, look at this place!" someone said. "Don't they ever clean up in here?"

She spent the rest of the time sitting there. She combed out her hair and wrapped her ankle, just in case. The door opened and closed, there were giggles and chatter and the sounds of music and people having fun, and she sat there. Where was Angela?

"You've been in there an awfully long time. Are you all right, dear?" A chaperone peeked under the door.

"I'm fine." Jennifer's heart sank. Damn. It had been automatic. Why hadn't she said she was sick?

"Well, come on out. There's nothing to be shy about.

"There must be plenty of people you know here," the woman screamed over the rock as she led her out to the dance floor. "Don't you see someone you know?" Jennifer shook her head. "Well, I'm sure you will."

Every time she tried to start back to the ladies' room she felt an eye on her. And there was the chaperone smiling reassuringly. Jennifer smiled weakly, leaned against a pillar, and reached for another paper cup of Coke. She peered over the rim.

Hardly anyone was dancing. Kids were either running through the mob on the dance floor or clustered in little groups screeching at each other over the noise. A few boys tried to climb up onto the stage where the DJ was screaming into the microphone and another bunch crawled under the tables, reaching up for potato chips. Someone put a handful of ice down another boy's shirt and in a second they were chasing through the crowds, weaving into the middle of the mob scene. Someone started tickling one of the girls. "Heee-hhhheeehhaaaaa . . ."

The music was deafening, blasting out over the up-roar.

"Wanna dance?"

"Wha?"

The boy in front of her had a Walkman stuck in his ear and was staring at her. She felt Dawn crunch behind her and put her hand back. They were still soggy.

"Wanna dance?"

"Yeah, yeah, yeah," the crowd screamed with the DJ. Suddenly the lights went out.

"Ooooooooooo!" rose from the crowd in the dark-ness. The lights flickered then came on.

"AAwwwwwwww!" the kids moaned.

They flickered out again and someone grabbed Jen-nifer from behind. She screamed and spun around.

"It's only me, Jen. Don't spaz."

Jennifer clutched her heart, gasping. "Angela! Don't do that!" she shrieked. "Where have you been?"

"I couldn't help it. Stacey wanted me to . . ."

The lights flickered again.

"What is that?"

"I don't know. Some nerds fooling around with the switches. They always try something weird. Honest, Jen, I tried to find you, but . . ."

"Wanna dance?" The boy was still there.

The rock pounded at them over the mike.

"How many places could I be?" Jennifer could hear herself shrieking over the noise. "How far could I go with . . ." She threw a glance at the boy. He was swaying and pitching to something on his Walkman. "Bom BA BA BABA," boomed out over the speakers. ". . . with these THINGS on my back?"

"I'm sorry, Jen. I said I was sorry. You don't have to scream at me, I tried to . . ."

The lights flickered. "OOOooooooooo."

The boy started to twitch. Suddenly one of his hands shot up into the air and he leaped. "POW!" he exploded.

"Who is he?" Angela yelled at her.

"How do I know?" she bellowed back.

"She doesn't want to!" Angela shrieked at him.

"Why aren't you dancing?" Samantha's voice cut in from somewhere. "Why don't you show us what you were doing out there, Jennifer?"

"Go away, Samantha," Angela intervened.

Samantha stared at the boy with the Walkman. He was shuffling back and forth in front of them. "Are you with him?"

The boy was jerking his head from side to side. Jennifer had nowhere to go. Dawn was already squashed against the pillar. He reached out and grabbed her. "Whoa!" yelled the boy and leaped into the air.

Jennifer felt herself hop up and pulled back. Her wings swayed. She felt herself lift off the ground. She reached back to hold them down.

"What is that?" Samantha snickered. "Another new dance? You are weird."

"Oh, come on, Sam. Leave her alone. I think it's pretty cool." That was David's voice.

Jennifer felt her wings slipping and grabbed them harder.

"No!" she yelled at the boy, but he was rocking wildly, his eyes closed, mouthing the words. Then the chaperone was standing before her smiling. "Contest," she said and winked at her.

"Huh?"

"You're in the dance contest," the chaperone shouted, smiling widely. Then she leaned in confidentially. "You see how much fun you can have when you try?"

"I'm in *what?*"

"Just go over there in the center so the judges can see you."

"Wow!" The boy grabbed her hand and pulled her away.

Jennifer's wings wobbled dangerously. "No!"

But behind them the crowd closed in. On the stage in front of them the disc jockey was putting on another record and the chaperones were smiling down. On one side of them, Stacey and David were flinging themselves down to the floor and then up again with a leap. "AY YA! AY YA!" blasted over the speakers above them. Stacey stopped bouncing just long enough to lean in. "Your ankle looks just great to me!" she hissed, then flung herself down again. Some girl in a blue skirt was stomping sideways, holding her arms up to her shoulders. And behind them the rest of the frantic contestants jerked and twitched and twisted. "Way O!"

"Whoa!" shouted her partner and leaped. Jennifer's wings jiggled. She reached back and caught the tips.

"Aw RIGHT!" the boy screamed and he reached back for his shirttails. He shuffled and twitched, his head tilted, singing to the ceiling.

". . . O . . . Way . . . O . . ." Onstage the disc jockey bent over his records and the mike shrieked and whistled.

Jennifer gasped for breath. Sweat was running down

her back and Dawn was getting away again. Any second now. It was going to happen. She waited for the screams and screeches. And still nobody screamed "WINGS!"

She focused her eyes on the stage. The chaperones were conferring, pointing at the dancers. One of them pointed at her. She looked away in agony. Oh, no.

"Just a minute!" One of the chaperones had gone to the mike. "Just a minute, everyone calm down now, we have some winners!" The crowd hushed suddenly, the music squealed to a stop. "Now," she leaned in to the mike and screamed at them, "when I point to you, please come up onto the stage to get your prizes. You were all wonderful, but we do have something special for . . ."

Jennifer shut her eyes and clenched her teeth.

"Now, the first prize goes to . . ." Jennifer's breathing stopped altogether. No, please, she begged. ". . . to the little girl in the blue skirt and the boy in the suspenders!"

A wild shriek rose from the crowd.

Jennifer let out her breath with a whoosh.

"Now, quiet, please, quiet down. The second pair of winners . . ."

No, please. She had never really prayed before.

". . . for the most unusual dance, is that girl in the green . . . what is it, a bow?"

"NO!"

Jennifer saw the boy's eyes look up into her hair. "YES!" He grabbed her. "That's you! We won! What do we get?" He shoved their way to the steps at the side of the stage and she stumbled up after him and almost tripped over the speaker wires. She pressed

Dawn against her tightly as he pulled her around the curtains and onto the stage.

She gasped. There were hundreds out there; hundreds of eyes staring up at her. When he let her go to get his prize, she shrank back against the curtain.

"No, don't go away, dear." The woman turned back to the microphone and shouted into it. "Now, would the winners" — the music started again with a crash and she screamed into the mike even louder — "show us their winning steps!"

Jennifer had to get out of there! The boy had leaped to the front of the stage and was holding on to his shirttails, shouting "Whoa!" as he sprang into the air. The girl in blue was twitching and stomping furiously.

Out on the floor it was pandemonium. They wouldn't notice her now. A group of boys ran snaking through the crowds in one direction and a lot of the kids had started dancing. She backed away, and Dawn brushed the curtains as she edged her way to the side. She was almost there. She heard a funny giggle or two and turned. Two boys were bent over something, giggling.

"One, two, three, PULL!"

The curtains closed with a swoosh. They picked her up and swooped her across the stage. There was a loud gasp from somewhere and she had just enough time to see a blur of open mouths and staring eyes before the curtain folds let her go. She shot across the stage feet first, slid into the wings on the other side, and was flung to the floor. From the other side of the curtain she heard a stunned hush, then a murmur of confusion. She scrambled to get up but was jerked back. Wires and ropes were twined around her legs and the Ace bandage was unraveling and wound up in them. She kicked at the writhing mess. The confusion out there was growing. People were shouting. She shook the ropes off her feet and pulled at the jumble of wires. The music whined to a stop.

"What the hell?" That was the DJ. "She pulled the plug out! What's she doing to my . . ."

"Are you all right?" The curtain flapped frantically. They were trying to get to her. "Answer me, dear . . . what's her name? Jennifer, answer me! Jennifer, are you all right, dear?" Jennifer tore at the Ace bandage.

"Someone open that curtain!"

"No, don't!" the chaperone screamed. "She might be caught!"

The curtain waved in a frenzy.

One last tug and she was free. She scrambled to her feet, leaped to the side of the stage and down the steps that led to the dance floor. She crouched low, panting. And dragging her wings over the steps she crept out as far as she could. It was chaos out there. People were scrambling up onto the stage and rushing across the floor. She could see David, Stacey, and Miranda standing in a group, motionless and staring, and Samantha, doubled over, laughing. She caught a glimpse of a white-faced Angela shoving her way through the crowd. Hundreds of heads were bobbing up and down, craning to see.

She crouched as low as she could. Now what?

The nearest table was only a few feet away. She had to make a dive for it. No one was looking in her direction; they were all glued to the stage. The paper tablecloth tore as she dove through. She crouched under the table, listening. But there were no cries of "There she is!" so she started crawling, her wings scraping the rough wood of the table above. She hardly felt it.

At the far end the tablecloth flopped almost down to the floor. She lifted it a bit and peered out. All the toes were pointing toward the stage. Once more she dove.

Safe.

From table to table she dove until she had circled the room and there were no more tables to go. Now she'd have to make a run for it. One, two . . .

She leaped from her hiding place, made a dash for the door, and turned the corner. She could imagine the roomful of people turning, hear a scream of "There she goes!" and thousands of feet pounding after her. But it didn't happen. She bounded up the stairs but it still wasn't fast enough! Her wings opened and she swooped up and around. At the top she touched down and listened. There wasn't a sound; only her own breath gasping, her heart pounding, Dawn trembling behind her. She leaned back against the wall and held on for a moment, eyes closed, panting, listening. Any minute now there'd be voices. She had to get out of there. She grabbed an umbrella off the stand and headed out into the yard. It was still pouring. She opened it just enough to make a little triangle over her head. Maybe she could wait on the church steps until it was over. Then, when her mother got there, she'd tell her what a great time she had . . . and . . .

Jennifer stared down the avenue. It looked dark and wet and empty with the rain streaming under the lamplights, splashing on the black street. There wasn't a soul in sight. Behind the church steps it was too dark, there were too many shadows. Her heart pounded against her chest; she had never been out alone like this before; she couldn't! She plunged out into the streaming rain and ran toward home, lunging alongside the buildings in the darkness.

# 16

## I Don't Want
## Them Anymore

Nothing worse could ever happen. She knew it. First
of all, her mother had been furious. "I told you I didn't
want you out in the street by yourself! How could you!
Don't you understand!" And Jennifer stood mute and
dripping. She couldn't explain.

There would be nothing more in her life. And no
one. Except for Angela.

Maybe she would become a bag lady.

She sat on her bed, head in hands. She twisted an
Oreo and it came apart. It looked like a checker piece
with a miniature skating rink on it. She stuck the top
back on and bit down. Black crumbs showered down
her front.

"What am I going to do when school starts? What
am I going to tell my father? How am I ever going to
do anything?"

"I don't know." Angela was trying to repair the wing
covers. "Classes are all right. But what about gym?
You could say you have some horrible disease or some-

thing." She looked up suddenly with a grin. "You'd make a great basketball player."

"Angela, it's not funny!" She picked up a pillow and threw it across the room. Angela looked at her stricken face and the grin disappeared. She quickly bent over her work again.

"These really are a mess." The pinks were bedraggled and tired-looking now. A sad shred of satin trim hung torn from the rest. "I guess we'll have to make new ones. At least this time we'll know what we're doing. Maybe we'll even put a ruffle on them. You could have a whole wardrobe of wing covers to match different outfits."

"I don't want new ones . . . I don't want any! Ange . . ." Jennifer felt the world stop as the question she'd been living with rose. She was suddenly so afraid. Thinking something was one thing, but when you said it aloud it became real. She took a very deep, shaky breath, then plunged in.

"Angela, do you think I'll ever not have wings again?" The last part came out in a rush.

Angela stared at her. She cocked her head, her eyebrows raised in the Cleopatra look. "What do you mean?"

"I mean," she paused as the fear rose higher, "what if I have to have them for the rest of my life?"

"Well?" She tilted her head further to the right. "So?" She didn't seem to grasp the significance of it. Jennifer grabbed her.

"Don't you get it? Don't you realize I'm probably the only person in the whole world with these things?" Her voice was rising. "I'm a mutant, forgodsake!"

"You're a what?"

"Mutant! A new evolutionary creature! A real weirdo!"

"Shh."

"And I don't know how to get rid of them! I don't even know how I got them!"

"Get rid of them?" Angela was horrified. "What? You can't do that!"

"That's what I'm afraid of."

"What are you talking about? They're wonderful!"

"Wonderful? You think what happened at the dance was wonderful?"

"Well, I . . ."

"Or the tree? Or the thing with the umbrella!" She fought for control of herself. Her voice lowered to a secretive whisper, as if she didn't want the wings to hear. "Angela, I don't think I want them anymore."

Angela gaped at her. "But . . ."

"Don't you realize what trouble they are? Do you know how many times in the last week you've said, 'Are you all right?' "

"But . . ."

"I'll probably never even get to wear one of those wedding dresses. Who'd want to marry someone with wings? They'd be afraid their kids would get 'em."

"But . . ."

But the words were pouring out of her now. "It's even hard taking a bath. I'll never see a movie again, or have a date — with anyone but you."

Angela looked up sharply but Jennifer didn't seem to notice. "And if a breeze comes along I have to be weighted down, forgodsake! And do you know the extra work I have to do? I'm lying to my mother all the time and she can't figure out what's going on and

I'll never show my face at school again . . . and I'm going to have to dress weird . . . and it's all because of" — she threw a hateful look behind her — "these!"

"But you can't get rid of them! Not yet! You need them for the Jennifer Jump!"

This time Jennifer stared. "Is that all you can think of? The Jennifer Jump? What about me?"

"It is you. You're the only one who can do it! Samantha will have a fit, she'll be so jealous. You'll even beat Penelope!"

"I don't care. Anyway, that's another thing. If I'm the only person in the whole world who can do it, aren't they going to wonder why? I'm not a great skater. I'm not even good. So why should I be able to do it if the champions can't . . . or Reggie!"

"How do you know? Maybe they just haven't thought of it yet."

"Oh, please!"

"Just wait, that's all. Then we can figure something out. It'll work, Jen. Trust me. I'll think of something."

"Don't you dare! Haven't you been listening to anything I said? I don't want them anymore. Read my lips, *I don't want them anymore!*"

"You mean now?"

The two girls confronted each other. Angela's mouth was wide open, her eyes staring.

"Have you tried?" she asked in awe.

Jennifer shook her head. "Not yet. I don't know how," she said. "You're the one with all the ideas. Think of something. How am I going to get rid of them?"

"Gee, I don't know." Angela fiddled with the chiffon, trying to pinch the torn part together. "In *The*

*Wizard of Oz* Dorothy just clicks her heels together to go home. Maybe you should try that."

"Oh, that's ridiculous."

"Well, can you think of anything?"

"No."

"Well?"

"Oh." Jennifer made her sick duck face but stood up anyway.

"You're supposed to have ruby slippers."

"Well, I don't. God, do I feel dumb!"

"Maybe your skates would do it."

"I will not! I feel enough like a jerk already."

But she was desperate. She stood in the middle of the room with her feet together. "I don't want wings, I don't want wings, I don't want wings." And she clicked her heels together three times.

Then she waited.

"Well?" She walked to the mirror. They were still there.

"Nothing," she said, disgusted. "Zilch. I can't believe I'm standing in the middle of the room clicking!" She was close to tears. She always was now.

"Well, you said to think of something, so I'm trying. I know! What would Alice in Wonderland do? First she went through the mirror, right? I mean, that's logical. You can see Dawn in the mirror, so maybe . . ."

"So maybe I'd shatter the glass and be maimed for life. I'm not Alice in Wonderland, Angela. I'm Jennifer Rosen and this is real life, not a stupid fairy tale!"

"Well." Angela put another pin in the satin ribbon. "I know! Voodoo! Don't they stick pins in dolls to make something happen? I read a book about a girl who almost got turned into a bird because of her wings. She sent for some stuff to rub on . . ."

"Angela . . ." There was a low warning in Jennifer's voice.

"Or, maybe you could soak them off." Jennifer looked up.

Five minutes later she was standing in the shower with the Shower Massage going full blast and aimed at Dawn. But it wasn't working. Her wings were only getting heavier and heavier by the second and soggier, hanging down her back like wet dishrags.

She moaned as she stepped out and dripped on the floor. "Now, how are we going to get them dry? It'll take forever." But Angela was already plugging in the hair dryer.

The hot air swooshed up and down her wings, hotter and hotter.

"Ow! You're burning me!"

"My arm's getting tired."

"Quit it, Angela. It hurts!"

So that had taken care of that and they were back where they had started. Jennifer was morose. "Now what?" she said. "Any other ideas?"

"Well, I don't know. Jen," — Angela hesitated before she said the words — "maybe, maybe you can't get rid of them. Maybe you're stuck with them."

"NO!"

"What's so terrible about it? You'd go on TV, right? Maybe they'd even make a movie about you."

"Angela."

"Well, maybe you're not the only one. Maybe you could put a secret code in the classifieds and join a club. 'Winged girl wants to meet others who share interests.' "

"*Get out!*"

Angela stared. "You mean it?" There was no answer; just a fixed, tortured stare.

Angela got off the cumpled bed and awkwardly gathered her things from the floor. She was very conscious of Jennifer, who was standing motionless, watching her as she swept them into her bag, then Angela hunted for her Reeboks under the bed. "Jen, maybe it isn't as bad as you think. Maybe . . ." But there was no response.

That had been hours ago. And Jennifer still didn't know what to do. She had sat on the edge of her bed for a long time staring, unseeing, and feeling the pain from the umbrella spoke in her wing. Angela had wanted to put a Band-Aid on it, but it would have hung in the air behind her and followed her. Besides, she was afraid it would tear the wing when they finally tried to take it off. So they'd left it alone. She felt terrible; Angela really did try to help.

Cleopatra had come to her, but when there was no response to her hopeful wag, she'd finally just crept under the bed and stayed there, her eyes looking up sorrowfully every once in a while as if trying to understand. Things weren't the way they used to be.

Her mother would come home soon. And she couldn't stand one more questioning look, another worried glance. She knew that she had called her father the night before, because she had overheard her on the telephone. "No, Henry, I don't think it's just because she's growing up. Something's wrong."

Everything was so tense.

She slumped and stared at her big toe. Maybe Angela was right. Maybe she should just tell her mother everything and get it over with. Maybe they should amputate. It couldn't be worse than this. It would probably be a relief.

Cleo stirred underfoot at the sound of her whimper. Her tail twitched for a second. But when there was no answering hand to stroke her head or ruffle her fur she merely shifted position and lay still.

There would be the *Enquirer*. GIRL SPROUTS WINGS.

She put on her nightgown and got into bed. At least she could pretend to be asleep when her mother got home.

## 17

# Stuck—Again!

"I'm so sick of everything."

Her mother looked up from her work. Jennifer stood in the doorway looking in. "Well," — she was concentrating on drawing a straight line — "why don't you call Angela and go do something. You haven't seen her for days." Her mother was still working on her project furiously. She said she was behind schedule and just had to push through.

"Why are you putting that mark there?"

"Jennifer." She put down the pencil and turned to look at her daughter across the room. "Honey, why don't you go skating? You were doing so much of it . . . I bet you're getting terrific!"

"I don't feel like it." She sounded sullen.

"Jennifer, you just can't brood about that dance forever. You're probably just imagining the whole thing, anyway, blowing it all out of proportion."

"I am not! You weren't there! How would you know?"

Her mother put down her ruler and swung around.

"I don't like your tone of voice, Jennifer. This is not, I repeat, not, appropriate behavior." Jennifer knew that her mother was annoyed but she couldn't go skating, not after throwing Angela out of the house. Angela was mad at her, too. But she needed her in order to go skating. Shoot, she needed her to go walking! And Angela wasn't even talking to her.

"You know you have a lesson coming up this week and the freestyles are just a couple of months away. I haven't spent all this money on lessons for the last five and a half years for you to lose interest now. And your father's talking about coming just to see you skate. Now, either you . . ."

"OK, OK, I'll go skating!"

"Please don't scream at me. And if you don't want to call Angela, call Stacey or Miranda. See if one of them wants to go. I'll call you at The Rink."

"You don't have to check up on me. I'm going!"

Her mother stared. "I wasn't," she said bitingly, "going to 'check up on' you. I was going to ask where you wanted to go for dinner, ribs or Chinese. But now, that's not appropriate!"

Jennifer felt awful again . . . still. Nothing, nothing was going right. She looked at her feet.

"Jennifer," her mother sighed deeply, "I know there's something bothering you. And I know you've had another fight with Angela. And I know that there are times when you have to work things out for yourself. But, I want you to know that I'm here. And I want to help." She sat waiting expectantly. But Jennifer just sort of collapsed inside and stood there.

"I know, Mom, thanks, but . . ." Her voice drifted away helplessly.

She backed out and left her mother there, grabbed

her gear from the closet, and left before they could get even further embroiled.

"Worse and worse and worse," she muttered as she stamped along next to the buildings. And now she had to go to The Rink. And she had to get Angela. "Damn." She was never going to be free.

Across the street from The Rink she headed for the phone booth on the corner, groped in her pocket for a quarter, and squeezed herself in. It was the old-fashioned kind, with doors on it, so at least no one would hear her. And she didn't have to stand there with her back sticking out for everyone to see. She closed the door behind her and dialed. The phone rang. She could just see it on the table in the foyer, ringing away in an empty apartment. What if she wasn't there?

"Wwrrrnngg. Wwrrrnngg" again. She hated this! "Wwrrrnngg." Please, let her be there, please. Then the sudden click as the receiver was lifted off the hook and a voice that sounded as if it belonged to a mouth full of peanut butter.

"Arroo?"

"Ange?"

"Ate a init." There was an audible attempt to swallow. "Ah oo aw wite? Weh are you?"

"Across from The Rink. I have to skate, but . . ." There was a pause. "Ange, I need you."

There was a tap on the door. Oh, no. A man stood outside, looking in. She shook her head at him and turned away. "Ange? You've got to come and help me with my wing covers."

"Now? I just got home from Stacey's." The peanut butter voice was gone. "Anyway, I thought you were mad at me."

"I have to skate. You don't have to stay. I can get them off, I just can't get them on."

"So you don't want me. You just need me for your . . ."

The man rapped his quarter against the glass. She looked at him, shook her head again, more violently this time, and deliberately turned her back.

"No, Ange. Please, I have to . . . my mother's gonna call to make sure I'm skating, and I can't even get on the ice without you."

"Oh, forgodsake, Jen, Mom wants me to go shopping with her. She says she never sees me anymore."

He tapped again. "Come on, kid, I've gotta use the phone!" Jennifer turned away again.

"Isn't there something else you can do?"

"No, Angela, that's what I'm trying to tell you. There isn't. I don't . . ." She looked up. The man had gone around to the other side of the booth and was pointedly staring at his watch. She turned away one more time, then casually leaned back against the doors.

It was the wrong move. She knew it the moment she did it. She felt the doors close tightly over a wing. Part of Dawn was clasped firmly between the two sections of the door. She'd done it again.

"Ange." There was no answer. Panic shot through her almost automatically. "Angela! Are you . . ."

"Jen?" The voice came mumbling and vague through the phone. "What's the problem? I was just taking a bite. I'll be . . ."

"I'm stuck!"

"Again! How?" It was almost a shriek.

"And there's a man outside who wants to get in."

"What?"

"He wants to make a call. He's making faces at me!"

"How did you do it this time?"

"I don't know. It's jammed in the door. Angela, I can't move!"

"You're not just saying this because you want to go skating?"

"No! Angela, get me out of here!"

"Oh, forgodsake, OK." But she sounded really annoyed. "I'll think of something to tell Mom and you just pretend to keep talking."

There was a loud crash as she slammed down the receiver. Jennifer winced.

Her wing pulled at her back. Furtively she put one hand behind her and tugged gently at it. But it was tightly pinched in. She twisted her neck around as far as she could. He was pacing now. She could see him come in and out of sight as he came into her line of vision then paced out again. She ducked her head and yammered loudly into the phone, nodding now and then, shaking her head furiously. Maybe he'd think she'd never hang up.

Suddenly his face pressed in on the glass of the booth and his mouth moved angrily. She swung back to the receiver. When she glanced up he was stalking furiously. He strode up and down a few more times, circled her, thrust his watch under his eyes, then threw up his hands. A boy in blue jeans stopped to watch, then moved on. Two ladies with dogs stopped to chat.

Across the street another phone booth emptied. He spotted it and ran, his briefcase banging against his legs. She watched him race between the cars, then leap for it. Too late. A woman slipped in just ahead of him. His head swung back on his neck, as if looking to heaven, then he spun around to look at Jennifer.

She could see his lips moving. Then he turned abruptly and hurried on down the street. The boy in jeans was gone. The women with the dogs were strolling away.

And it seemed very, very still.

She tried to shift a little. But it was no use. It was hard standing so still for so long. She was going to suffocate. It was getting hotter and hotter with no air. And it smelled bad. She tried to take a deep breath. She could hardly move.

Her eyes traveled around the phone booth. It was a narrow glass box. Outside, just behind her on the street, a stream of cars moved along. And down the block, on the avenue, people were going along, going somewhere, doing things. They weren't paying any attention to her. She tried to shift again.

Where was Angela? She couldn't stand it!

She had to do something.

She put her hands up behind her, felt her wing, and tugged cautiously. Nothing. Zilch.

She pressed her hand on one side of the door and tentatively pushed at it. It was jammed tight. One hand wasn't going to do it. If she could push and pull at the same time, maybe. She let the receiver drop and dangle on the end of its silver coil as she reached back with both hands. It put a strain on her wing stem, and she felt her wing squeezed in the crack of the door pulling one way as she pulled the other. It was unbearable.

She let her arms swing forward again and felt the release of pain. She waited, breathless, until the sharpness subsided, then put her hands slowly behind her and tried again, one hand pulling on the wing, the other pushing at the door.

This time she thought it would rip. She tried to keep her back as close to the door as she could, but as she reached back and pressed against it, her back arched involuntarily and the trapped wing pulled at its stem again. She would have to let go.

One more second! She could stand one more second! She gritted her teeth and could hear herself squeezing out the sounds of pain. She pressed one more time.

The door flew open. She was propelled from the booth and shot backward.

She sat for a long time, feeling the pain recede, staring at the empty booth. She had done it. Herself! A sudden triumph surged through her.

She was halfway across the street when Angela jogged around the corner.

"I thought you were stuck," she panted accusingly. "You scared me for nothing."

"I was stuck."

"What happened?" She was breathless as she ran alongside.

"Some man wanted to get in and I thought if I leaned against the door he'd be afraid I'd fall out so he wouldn't . . ."

"Forget it!" She was panting. "What are you running for?" Jennifer was racing, her eyes on The Rink's door, her feet barely touching the ground. "You'd better be careful, before you take off!" Jennifer reached for the door and flung it open. "But how'd you get out?"

"I don't know. I just pushed and . . . I did it myself, Angela!" She was running up the stairs, pounding at them. Angela slowed down, panting, and finally gave up. Jennifer left her behind. Her heart was racing as she pushed at the door.

Don was at the desk bent over the schedule book. Other than that the place was empty.

"You back again?" He barely looked up as Jennifer dashed past him and headed for the bathroom. Angela appeared, staggering, at the top of the stairs. "Brought your cohort, huh?" Don added as she ran in after her.

Jennifer didn't even bother to change her clothes. She shuffled in her bag for the pinks and shoved them into Angela's hands.

"Honestly, Jen, what's wrong with you?" she demanded as she fumbled with the pins.

"Nothing."

"I came, didn't I?"

"I know."

"So?" She followed as Jennifer pushed the door open and headed out to put on her skates. She tugged at the slip knot and the laces fell apart as if by magic. She whipped them up, loosening them into a chaos of string, then violently thrust her foot into the boot. Her fingers flew as she did it up and started working on the other. She threw her booties on the bench, grabbed her gloves, and headed for the ice. Angela was still struggling into her skates.

"Hey, wait for me!"

But she didn't.

She pushed out onto the ice. Oh, it felt good. She whipped around the rink, feeling it glide under her. Her wings flat, her arms outstretched, she turned and led herself into a waltz jump. Her wings opened slightly on it and she entered her own world. She did another. It was wonderful, almost like flying. She forgot everything. She rounded the rink once or twice then, then bent into the arabesque. She felt the Jennifer Jump coming. She bent her knee deeply, straightened it slowly, and lifted. How many times had she done this? She leaned into it; it was almost automatic. She felt the music behind her; powerful, swelling music that lifted her, forced her to let the ice fall away beneath her. One, two, three, up . . . one, two, three, down. The music ebbed and softened. It pulled her down. She landed, folded her wings smoothly, and went onto her outside edge to make the turn at the far side of the rink. Then she simply lowered her back leg, straightened her body, and looked straight into the astonished face of Penelope.

Behind her, Angela was openmouthed in horror.

# 18

## The Accident

"How'd you do that?"

Jennifer didn't have a voice. "I . . . I . . . What?" she sputtered.

"That jump. How'd you do that?"

"Ohmagod!" Jennifer stared at Angela in desperation. "Wha . . . wha . . ."

Angela slid in between them. "Do what?" she asked lightly.

"That jump! I've never seen anything like it!" Penelope's voice was alive with excitement. "It was wonderful! What was it?"

"What jump?" Angela looked so innocent, so eagerly curious. Penelope swiveled from one of them to the other and her own eagerness ebbed visibly. "I should have guessed you wouldn't tell me," she said. Then she turned abruptly. Jennifer watched her skate away. She had sounded so angry and resentful and, Jennifer felt a terrible twinge inside her, hurt. She felt like another Samantha.

"You were supposed to be the lookout," she hissed

at Angela furiously. "You did it again! You did it again!"

"You didn't wait!" Angela hissed back. But Jennifer wasn't listening. She was watching Penelope race round and round, attacking the ice with each powerful stroke. "She thinks we're being mean on purpose."

"Maybe she'll think she imagined it."

"She will not!"

Penelope had gone to the far end of the rink and had sunk onto the ledge, bending over her skates as if she were retying them. Impatiently she brushed at something on her cheek, then bent over again, fumbling with the laces.

Jennifer couldn't stand it. She started toward her.

"What do you want?" Penelope's eyes were glittering.

"I . . . uh . . ." Jennifer felt terrible. "We didn't mean to be mean." She didn't know what else to say.

"You know that was a jump."

"Oh, that. I don't know what it was. It just sort of happened."

"Nothing like that just happens. It was amazing." She stopped suddenly and stared as if she had just noticed something strange. "What are those things on your back?"

"Oh." Jennifer had a sinking feeling. She had forgotten them. "These?"

"Yes. What are they?"

Jennifer tried to sound nonchalant. "They're for my costume," she said. "I thought I should practice with them on." It sounded lame, even to her.

"Your costume? I don't believe it. What kind of costume?"

"She's skating to 'On the Wings of a Dove.' " Angela had come up behind them.

"Oh." Penelope looked blank. "I never heard of that one."

"It's an old song," Angela hurried to explain. "Her mother sings it all the time. I guess it's really old. You wouldn't know it."

"Oh, so you need wings?"

"Yeah. I'm the dove." When she tried to make her sick duck face it felt stupid and she gave it up. But Penelope wasn't even watching. She was thinking.

"When you did that jump," she said very slowly, as if she were trying to figure something out, "they went . . . up."

Jennifer and Angela looked at each other.

"What went up?"

"Those." She pointed at the limp pinks drooping halfway to the ice.

"They did? Oh, hey, they did." Jennifer was watching her blade push snow into designs on the ice.

"That's pretty cool. How do you work them?"

"See." Angela jumped in again. "We put strings here and connected them to her wrists, so when she moves her arms, they go up. See? Show her, Jennifer."

Jennifer glowered. An all too familiar feeling was gripping her. A little voice in the back of her mind was saying, Keep out of this, Angela, but she raised her arms and her wings little by little, simultaneously, very slowly, to be sure they were synchronized.

"I don't see any strings."

"They're threads, really. They're almost invisible." Jennifer choked. Something else was going out of control. She could feel it. She had to get out of there.

"I've got to get home for dinner," she said abruptly. "Come on, Angela."

"But . . ."

"Come on, Angela." She spaced her words pointedly, "Or your mother said there's going to be trouble."

"Wait." Penelope sprang after them. "Wait just one minute, please. Show me how to do it. Just once, OK?"

Angela shrugged and leaned in to Jennifer. "Do it without Dawn," she whispered. "Then it won't work and we'll be off the hook."

"I will not. I'll kill myself," she whispered back. She glanced at Penelope standing nearby, watching them. She was waiting expectantly.

"Really, Penelope, I can't. I don't know what I did."

"Well, how did it start?" The eagerness was back in her voice. "How were you standing? Were you on an outside edge or . . ."

"I really don't know."

"Well, let me figure this out. Let's see . . ." Penelope got into position. "Now, if you start a forward glide," she said as she started to walk through the motions. "One, two three," she murmured to herself, "now, bend the knee, arabesque, and," she paused, "lift." She stopped and turned to the girls. "Then you have to keep going and land on the same foot. How'd you do that?" She was completely puzzled. "I don't get it," she said aloud. "I can only go up on the lift. How do you go forward, too?"

"I don't know. I told you that." Jennifer's heart was thumping again.

"Maybe you're seeing things." Even Angela was panicking.

"Why are you so nasty, Angela? I wasn't seeing

things. And I'm not trying to steal your jump, if that's what you're worried about. Maybe if I pick up speed."

"No, Penelope, don't try it. Please. It's not what it looked like."

"I just want to see if I can do it. It's a great jump. And if you can do it I guess I can."

Jennifer looked at Angela helplessly. "I knew this was going to happen; I knew it, I knew it." She turned on her. "Why do I ever listen to you?"

"I didn't do anything! You came on the ice and . . ."

But behind them Penelope was starting the forward skating. She was going too fast.

Her glides were long and strong, powerful across the ice. She made the turn once, moving faster and faster to pick up the speed she would need to carry her forward. She made the last turn, then bent slowly into it. She was heading toward the windows! It was going to happen!

"Penelope, don't!"

Jennifer sprang after her. But Penelope was already leaning into the arabesque, one leg high above her head, her body arched into that beautiful, familiar, flowing arc. She bent her supporting leg deeply, then threw her body forward.

"No! Turn!"

In midair the pose shattered. Her legs thrust back under her and her toe pick caught the ice. Her body pitched forward. She couldn't stop! She put her hand out to stop the fall.

The windows!

Jennifer sprang forward and grabbed for her.

She felt the crash, felt the glass splinter around them, heard the screams echo, then felt Dawn open as they plunged through.

Jennifer caught Penelope and held on.

Penelope was a dead weight falling. They plummeted, the blur of the trees rushed by. She held on and forced Dawn open as wide as she could. Her wings weren't strong enough to fly with them both but the blur of the backyards coming up at her slowed. She banked and just missed one of the brick walls, then swerved past the tree trunk. The ground was spinning up faster again. She had to keep them open. She saw the ground, tensed, and prepared to hit. They were hurled to the ground and lay motionless.

Jennifer knew they were down. She stirred and felt a heavy weight. Penelope was limp and heavy and tangled up with her. Jennifer moved and groaned. She heard other screams and looked up. She was confused. She tried to find out where the noise was coming from. Don was leaning out of a shattered window and looking down on her. "Jennifer!" It came from far away. She closed her eyes for a second. When she looked up again he had disappeared. Then there was a moan. She knew it wasn't hers. Another shout.

She could move. And slowly she disentangled her leg from the heavy weight and carefully drew herself out from under it. She sat, bewildered, feeling nothing, and stared at the body next to her. There was another shout from somewhere far away.

"Penelope?"

She leaned over and touched her. Penelope moved her head, rocking it slowly over the ground.

"Penny?"

A soft moan answered her. Then Penelope's eyes opened and her lips moved. "You were right. I shouldn't have tried it." Then her eyes closed again.

From behind them Jennifer was aware of commotion. It surrounded them. There were people — familiar people with strange, terrified faces — hands holding her, voices telling her not to move, questions she couldn't understand.

"I'm all right," she murmured and staggered up to prove it.

"They're alive!"

She couldn't quite make out what everyone was saying, and she backed away from them all. She felt someone help her to one of the stone benches in the garden and wondered about the two motionless birds that seemed to be drinking at a little pool in front of her. She heard some words, isolated words, and was vaguely aware of her skates being taken off. She was beginning to ache. Her wings felt as if they'd been crushed and broken. She tried to stand up but heard someone say, "No, dear, just keep still." Then she was aware of people turning away from her and toward Penelope.

Jennifer tried to see Penelope but it was hard. Penelope was hidden behind a circle of people and Jennifer could only see parts of her between them.

When she saw Penelope's hand move there was a slight shifting from the crowd, an almost imperceptible stirring. And Jennifer took a quick gulp of air. Penelope was conscious.

In the distance a barely audible sound wailed. It swelled in the streets beyond the brownstone buildings, then stopped. Ambulance. A terror-filled "No!" escaped Jennifer. It was barely a whisper. They were going to find out! She had to get away.

Everyone was focused on Penelope. No one was paying any attention to her.

She slowly got off the bench. Keeping her eyes on

the crowd she inched her way to the wall and the open door. No one saw her.

She turned.

For the first time she forgot about the wing covers. Oblivious to everything, she staggered out through the house and onto the street. She turned, aching, limping, running past the crowds, the waiting ambulance, faster, faster toward home.

"Jen! Jen!"

She shook Angela off and kept going. Breathless she pushed on, across the streets, down the blocks, her wings heavy and limp against her back as she ran. Angela kept up with her but Jennifer hardly knew it or cared. In the elevator a strange woman stared at her. Angela put her arm around Jennifer protectively as the woman took a step toward them. "Are you all right?"

"She's just upset," Angela explained while Jennifer stood rigid, her eyes fixed on the door. Her stomach ached from holding in her cries.

When the elevator door opened they rushed out, running through the hallway to her door. She struggled with her keys in the lock and fell in as the door swung open.

Then she burst into tears.

# 19

# *Telling Her Mother*

"I don't want them anymore!" Jennifer screamed.

She was sobbing and the words were half smothered by the other sounds coming out of her throat.

"I don't want them!"

"What is it?" Her mother looked from Angela to Jennifer and then back again. "What happened?"

At the sound of her mother's voice Jennifer choked. She ran to her room and slammed the door behind her.

Her mother looked at Angela. "What's going on?" There was a long pause. "Did you two have another fight?"

Angela shook her head dumbly and looked at her hands. "I can't . . ."

"Angela, what's happened? Something's going on and I want to know what it is."

She looked at her helplessly. From the other room the sobs were muffled and violent. The two heads swiveled toward the closed door. "OK, Angela, I think

I'd better hear this from the horse's mouth. You're off the hook." And Angela made her escape. "Tell her I'll call her later!" she called as she fled.

Then Jennifer's mother pushed back her hair and closed her eyes for a moment, as if preparing herself, knocked on the door, and entered her daughter's room.

Jennifer lay across the bed. "I don't want them," she wept as she punched the pillow. "I don't want them!"

"Don't want what, sweetheart?" She slipped onto the bed next to her daughter and stared at the bedraggled wing covers emerging from her daughter's heaving back. Jennifer felt the weight on her bed shift. "Please tell me what's wrong."

"And I can't get rid of them . . . and," she gulped, "I don't know what to do!"

"Get rid of what?"

But Jennifer just kept going as if her mother weren't there. "When I first got them I thought they'd be sorta fun . . . then I thought they'd make me special . . . but I'm not! I'm still just di-different." She hiccupped and felt her eyes filling again and spilling over. "I'm more than different. I'm strange!" The word came out in a wail.

"What are you talking about?"

"And Penel . . . Penel . . . Penelope!"

"What about Penelope?"

But there were only the wails and sobs that dissolved into a whole series of hiccups, and then, "If she dies, it's all my fault!"

"Jennifer Rosen, I want to know what's going on — now! What are you talking about?"

"My . . . my . . ." And then it burst out of her from

deep inside. "My wings!" she screamed. "My wings!"

Beyond her own sobbing she became aware of silence.

"Wings?" Her mother's face was a blank. Jennifer felt her soft hand calming her down, making little circles on her back above the wings. And she clutched her mother's arm and just held it. As closely as she could.

After a while her mother's voice came through the fog. "Wings?" she said again. Her voice was puzzled and wondering. "Why don't you just take them off?"

Jennifer looked up. Her wing covers were still on her back. She had a sudden glimpse of herself running through the streets with them wobbling behind her. "I can't," she moaned.

"Well, here, let me help you."

"Not those." She was miserable. "The real ones."

"Wings?" Her mother's voice was soft with control. Jennifer nodded and gulped. "Wings," she said.

Her mother touched the bedraggled wing covers gently. And then the phone rang.

Her mother sighed. "It happens every time," she complained and waited for it to stop. But it just kept ringing, stopped, then started again. Reluctantly she got up to answer it.

"Yes, she's here." Jennifer could hear it clearly. Her mother sounded puzzled. "Yes, she's all right. Upset about something but, no, I don't think she's hurt." Then a sudden anxiety. "Why?"

There was a long pause, until a shocked exclamation sent Jennifer diving into the pillows, feeling the tears squeezing through her fingers and into the sheets. "What! . . . But! . . . OH, MY GOD!"

Jennifer lay frozen, eyes closed against the images

that swam in her mind. Then she heard the horrible question in a shaking voice, "How is she?" And Jennifer waited endlessly for the next whispered sound, "Oh, I'm so glad. Yes, I'll tell her."

When she looked up her mother was standing in the doorway, white and shaking.

"She's going to be all right," she said and leaned heavily against the bed. "You went out the window?" Her voice was incredulous.

"That's what I was trying to tell you."

"Oh, my God. Oh, Jen." She sat down as if her legs couldn't hold her up anymore. Neither of them spoke.

"Well," said her mother, finally, when she could, "that was the police. They were very upset when they couldn't find you."

"I couldn't," whispered Jennifer. "The wings." Her mother nodded. Then Jennifer had to know. "Penelope?"

"There were a couple of broken bones and a bad concussion." Jennifer stifled a cry as her eyes filled with horror.

"But she's . . ."

Her mother reached out for her. "Jen, it's all right. Bones heal. Really." Again the room was filled with a deep silence. Then, "They said it was a miracle. You went out a window?"

Only a tiny nod answered her. "Jen, I want a doctor to see you."

"NO!" Her answer was explosive with terror.

It seemed forever before either of them moved. Each stared into space, motionless, until her mother's voice finally stirred the silence.

"OK, Jen. Now," she reached out gently, "I'll tell

you what. I'll make a pot of tea and suppose you tell me all about your . . . wings."

Tea was her mother's remedy for everything: colds, not being able to sleep, just being upset. It arrived hot and steaming and fragrant at all the right, comforting times. "Here, blow." She handed Jennifer a tissue. Jennifer blew her nose hard, then sat up sniffling.

She followed her mother into the living room, sat down at the table in the dining area, and watched her slow, deliberate actions as her mother went through all the familiar motions: putting on the flame, running the water, and then putting the pot on the stove. She reached up to the top shelf of the cupboard and brought down the Oreos. She put the package on the table so Jennifer would know that everything was normal. She put the honey on the table and her grandmother's teaspoons. Jennifer noticed that her mother's hands were shaking. She sniffled and stifled a little sob again. Her mother was scared, too.

The tangy scent of Cinnamon Rose Tea drifted up as Jennifer stared into the cup. Penelope was going to be all right. She had to take it in. Slowly she dipped her spoon into the thick honey and watched it drip. She twisted it and the honey dribbled, coiling into the cup. She stirred the tea, swirling it around, then cradled the mug in her hand. It made her feel cozy and warm.

Her mother slid onto the chair next to her and took a quick sip of tea.

"Hot," she said and pushed the cookies toward Jennifer. Jennifer took one and twisted it open. She licked halfheartedly at the icing.

"Now," her mother said, looking anxiously into Jennifer's red and aching eyes, "tell me about these wings."

"Well," Jennifer closed her eyes for a moment, "do you remember those pencils you gave me?"

"Pencils?" Her mother looked blank. "I think so. What have they got to do with it?"

So she told her. Gulping and sniffling and sometimes letting loose a little sob, she told her all that had happened: how she had gotten the wings, all the problems she had had, how she'd been afraid to tell anyone.

"Except Angela," her mother said. Jennifer looked to her sheepishly and nodded.

Staring into her cup of tea, she told her about the flying disaster.

"Flying?"

Jennifer couldn't even look at her.

And the dance, and having to cut up all her clothes, and how now she was afraid she would have to have them forever.

Every once in a while she glanced up. But the expression on her mother's face sent her staring back into her tea. When she told her about cutting up the negligee, she thought she saw her mouth twitch.

"So," her mother said, "that's what those are," and she nodded at the pinks on her daughter's back. "I thought they looked familiar."

Jennifer nodded, subdued.

"Don't you want to take them off?" her mother asked and Jennifer looked up, startled. Her heart started thumping again. Now her mother would know for sure.

"I . . ."

"Come on, turn around."

Very gently her mother undid the safety pins, one by one, and the wing covers slipped off. They fluttered to the ground and lay motionless. "I can't see anything."

"I told you. They're invisible. You can't see them except in a mirror. That's another thing," she sighed. "I have to go around avoiding every mirror in the world."

"Can I touch them?"

"I guess so." She sat as still as she could and felt her mother's cool, trembling hand touch the base of her wing where it came out of the now ragged hole in her sweatshirt.

"Oh, my goodness," her mother said weakly, "you really do have something back there. I . . . uh . . . I think I have to sit down."

She sat with a little plop and sank back, gazing at her Jennifer, speechless. Then a faint, understanding smile touched her face. She shook her head slowly as she looked at her daughter.

Jennifer nodded. "See? It's been awful," she whispered. "And then, today, it was the pits. Penelope . . ." Again her eyes filled with tears. "Penelope . . ."

"How on earth did Penelope get involved? I thought you didn't like her."

Jennifer shook her head. "No, she's sorta nice, just shy. It was all my fault. If I hadn't invented the Jennifer Jump it never would have happened."

"The Jennifer Jump?"

Jennifer stopped. She had forgotten how little her mother knew about what was going on in her life. She didn't even know about the Jennifer Jump. "Oh, it's this impossible jump. Maybe one of the Olympic champions could do it, or Reggie. But I'm not sure."

She saw her mother's eyebrows raise. "But you can do it?"

"Yeah. Because of, you know, them." A skeptical

look crossed her mother's face. "See, it's this jump where you take off on one . . ." She slid sideways off her chair and went to the middle of the floor. Skating was always awkward on the rug. She really couldn't glide. But she jabbed at the rug a few times, then went into her arabesque. Somehow off the ice it always wobbled. She fluttered. And up she rose. There was no momentum to take her more than a few inches, but even in the living room and on the rug it was the Jennifer Jump.

"That's not quite right," she said apologetically, "but you get the idea. It's . . ." She looked up and saw her mother's face, then dove into the couch, hiding her head in the pillows. She felt the tears threatening again.

There was a light hand on her back. "Oh, Jennifer, oh, baby." Then, with a shaky smile, as she shook her head again, "You've really been through it, haven't you?"

Jennifer nodded in the pillows.

"But why didn't you tell me?"

Her voice was muffled. "I was so afraid. I didn't know what to do. I thought maybe, you'd want to . . . amputate."

"Amputate? Oh, sweetheart." Her mother reached out and drew her close. "Does it hurt if I hug a couple of wings?"

"Wait." Jennifer lifted her wings to let her mother's arms slide in under them. "That's better," she sighed and snuggled close. Hugging was wonderful.

There was a long, comfortable silence before her mother pushed her back and looked at her. "Well, Jennifer, I don't know. All I can say is, Thank God it's just wings."

Jennifer sat straight up. "Huh?"

"Oh, honey." There was another long, shaky pause. "I was afraid something really terrible was going on."

"Terrible! You don't think this is terrible? You don't think having wings is terrible?" She could hear her voice rising in hysteria again. "What could be terrible?"

"Oh, Jen, I don't know. Drugs or . . ." She stopped at the stunned disbelief on Jennifer's face.

"Me? Oh, Mom, that's dumb! You know I'd never do that. Me?"

"Oh, Jen, I'm sorry. I just didn't know what was going on. I knew there was something and every time I tried to talk to you about it you . . . and you know my imagination!" The sob turned into a sheepish little laugh. "It wasn't big enough for this, though." She gave her a little squeeze and they smiled tremulously at each other. "Just tell me one thing, Jenny." Jennifer drew back as apprehension gripped her. "Does this mean you're not going to do the ironing anymore?"

Jennifer giggled and snuggled in again. Suddenly her wings didn't seem so bad, not if her mother could smile.

"Now, tell me about Penelope. What happened?"

Jennifer's heart went thump again. She got up and went back to the table. She dipped the sticky spoon into the honey and watched it dribble back into the jar. It made spirals on the golden surface. Then she started. When she had finished telling her mother all about it her mother hugged her close. Jennifer buried her head in her shoulder.

"It was all my fault," her voice was muffled. Her mother's hand stroked her hair softly. "No, Jen, it wasn't."

"It was. If it hadn't been for the Jennifer Jump it never would have happened."

"And if you hadn't known you could fly you never could have saved her. I'm so proud of you, Jen. Petrified, but proud."

"Really?"

"Really."

A very thin coating was left on Jennifer's spoon. She licked it off. There was one more thing she had to know and her heart began to pound again. "Mom."

"Yes?"

She swallowed hard and paused. "Mom, do you think I can ever get rid of them? Without amputating?" She rushed the last words before her mother had a chance.

Her mother sighed. "I don't know, sweetheart. I haven't had any experience with this kind of thing before. But . . ." Jennifer held the spoon up to the light. The sunbeams shot off the edges. "I'm not rushing you to the operating room, so don't worry about that now." A wonderful relief swept through her. "And, I'll bet there's a way. Somehow." Jennifer was concentrating hard. "If you got 'em, there must be a way to unget 'em. You know, Jen, there's an old saying, 'If something goes up it's got to come down.' " She sat back and shook her head slowly again. "Oh, honey, I just can't believe it."

She laughed a little and then, "You know, I'm a little jealous. Where did you say you put those pencils?"

That night Jennifer reached up for a long, satisfying good-night hug for the first time in a long time.

"Sleep tight, sweetheart," whispered her mother. "Sweet dreams."

"Stay with me?" Jennifer's voice was soft and pleading, the way it had been when she was little.

"All right." Her mother sat down on her window seat and looked out at the sky. "It's a funny thing," she said in the quiet night, "Penelope said something about dreaming that she was flying. When I called her mother she said Penelope doesn't remember much. But she said she dreamed that you saved her. And you did, you know. You really did."

Jennifer reached down, as usual, and touched her wings. They shifted slightly against her legs as she changed her position and brushed her lightly. She'd never be able to lie on her back again, she thought drowsily. She gazed past her mother's dark silhouette and out at the moon. If she wanted to, she thought, she could be out there, silently sailing over the city, in the darkness. If she wanted to, she could fly out, sailing, sailing, and touch the moon, dance on it.

Cleopatra settled down on the floor next to the bed. Jennifer could hear her tags tinkling as she stretched out, her head on her paws.

Everything was normal.

On the table next to her bed was the self-portrait without wings. Whatever goes up, she thought, has to come down. Everything was going to be all right.

And she fell asleep.

# 20

## They Go

A bell was ringing.

Deep within a dream it had started a rhythmic calling.

Jennifer shifted slightly.

She was balanced on a buoy on a gently moving sea. She had been there forever. But there was room on the buoy for only one foot and so she leaned over the sea in a perfect arabesque, watching the heavy, slow water swell up under her and tip her down toward the waves, then ebb and tip her up toward the sky. Over and over again.

Off in the distance an island was rising. It grew, drifting toward her. Hazy figures were dancing on the black rocks. They were having so much fun she wanted to join in. Her eyes followed it but she could only bob up and down on her buoy. As the island came close and the dancers tipped up and down, in and out of her sight, she poised, ready to leap.

The ringing sounds were louder now, shrill. They

pushed aside the island and the sea and centered, loud and compelling, calling her up from her dream.

"It isn't finished yet!"

She opened one eye.

A brilliant morning, swimming between the slats of the venetian blinds, dazzled her. Her eyes closed against it.

It was the telephone ringing, not the buoy. Why didn't her mother answer it?

"Bbbrrrrnnnnnggg, bbbrrrrnnnnnggg."

She lay waiting to sink back into that warm, rhythmic sleep. She wanted her dream back. She wanted to tell it what to do. "Bbbbrrrngg." The bell pushed the few remaining, suspended fragments of her dream beyond reach. Gone.

She opened her eyes again and stared overhead, coming back to herself. Above her there was a note on the bulletin board.

*Took Cleo out. Be back in a minute. Your orange juice is by your bed.*

She reached for the juice, pushed back the covers, then padded sleepily into the hall.

"Ello?" She took a sip of the juice. It was fresh and cool going down through her.

"Jen! You're gonna be on TV! Put on channel four! Hurry!"

"Huh?" Her eyes snapped open.

"Put on channel four! You're . . ."

The receiver hit the floor and bounced a few times.

". . . Hank Christopher . . ."

". . . and this is Marilyn Haywood with the story of a miracle in today's headlines; the story of two young teenage girls who fell from a second-story window and not only survived, but . . ."

Jennifer froze. She hardly noticed when her glass of orange juice tipped and dribbled down her front. On the screen was The Rink — the narrow stairs going up, the desk where Don sat, the white rink. Then the camera zoomed across the ice and past the broken window and into the backyard as if it were falling. It was a blur. She clutched at the chair, suddenly dizzy.

Then it showed a glimpse of Penelope, smiling weakly, but smiling from a hospital bed. ". . . escaped with a bad concussion, a broken arm and ribs, and a few cuts and bruises. But with all this it is a miracle that she is alive. They'll be watching her for a few days, but soon this brave girl will be back on the ice as good as new." The camera focused on Penelope's mother, smiling and nodding tearfully. "We have not as yet been able to contact the other girl, a Jennifer Rosen, who seemed not to have been hurt at all in this miraculous fall, but we hope for an exclusive interview sometime today." The commentator swiveled to face another camera. "And now for the national news. There was a fire in . . ."

Jennifer turned away and stumbled toward the hall. A distant voice was calling her. "Jen . . . Jen . . ." The sound was faint but real. She stared wonderingly at the phone, still leaning cockeyed against the floor. "Jen . . . Jen?" She picked it up slowly.

"Angela?"

"Did you see it?" Angela was beside herself with excitement. "You're famous!"

"Angela, I can't believe it! It's awful. How did they find out?"

"I don't know. Someone musta called News Hotline. You're famous! She even said you saved Penelope!"

"Angela, did you? If you . . ."

"It wasn't me, I swear I didn't! Look, I'm coming over."

"It's the worst thing that ever happened to me!"

"I'll knock in sequence, like a code, you know, so you'll know it's me. I've got it all figured out. It's like my name, see, An-ge-la, see, Boom-be-boom. Got it?"

Jennifer slammed down the phone.

She spun to the mirror and looked hard. They were still there, drooping apologetically, sort of flopped over at the tips and a little crinkled where they'd been crushed. And they still ached.

Somewhere in the back of her mind she had always thought that if she told her mother, they'd disappear somehow and it would all end. She didn't know why she had thought that, but she had.

But it hadn't happened. They were still there.

"Damn." She closed her eyes for a moment and shivered.

She was still there, staring numbly into the mirror, when the keys rattled in the lock.

"Cleo, stop it! How can I take your leash off if . . ." The door opened and Cleo tumbled in, wiggling. "Jennifer, I . . . Cleo, stop it!" Her mother leaned over the bounding dog, fumbling with the leash. "Cleo, sit!"

Obediently the dog sat, her long tail swishing on the rug as Jennifer's mother bent over to take the leash off. "I picked up some lox and bagels, sweetheart. I thought we needed a treat." There was a forced cheeriness in her voice. "But there's something . . ." She paused as she stood up and turned toward her. "Jennifer, honey, there's something I have to tell you." She stopped.

Two big tears were rolling down her daughter's face. She came up behind her and looked deeply into the reflection, put her head to one side, and listened. The television was faint in the other room.

"You know."

Jennifer nodded. In the mirror the wings bobbed sadly up and down. "Angela called."

"Oh, honey, I'm sorry."

She reached out for her and Jennifer lifted her wings to let her mother's arms slide in under them.

"What am I going to do? Now everybody will know."

"No, they won't, sweetheart. All they'll know is that you had a fall and you're OK." She was smoothing down her hair.

"But they will know when I go . . . if I . . ." She stopped. "I'll never go out again."

"Sshhh, it'll work out somehow."

"How?"


"I'm never going out again."

Jennifer was talking to herself. She dragged herself into the kitchen and opened the refrigerator door. Nothing looked good. She pulled open the freezer door, reached for a raspberry ice, and tore at the carton. The ragged edges of the cardboard hung in shreds as she grappled with it inside the freezer. As she tore at the paper she changed her mind. She didn't want it. She didn't want anything. It landed, half wrapped, on the ice cube tray. It would stick and turn the ice cubes pink. But it didn't matter; she didn't care. Nothing mattered. She hadn't been out for a week.

At first there had been the phone calls. Her father's voice was panicked. "Are you all right? It was on the news here. What happened?" But she couldn't bring herself to tell him the whole story.

Reggie called and Penelope's mother and all the kids from school and the newspeople. Her mother told them all that she was resting and no, they weren't going to sue. And yes, Jennifer was fine.

"She's had a shock," she said through the crack in the door to the reporters who waited there, their floodlights streaming across the floor each time she opened it. Even Jennifer's mother hardly went out, except to walk the dog. They were afraid to go out to the store. And they were getting sick of ordering pizza and Chinese every night.

Even David had called. "Wow!" he said, awe and longing in his voice. "When you're feeling better, wanna go for a bike ride or something?"

"Sure, sometime."

"Can't you just see it!" she had sneered at Angela. "I'd probably take off, bike and all, like Miss Gulch. And she turned into the Wicked Witch of the West!"

Angela was getting tired of just hanging around. Stacey wanted her to go roller-skating, school had started and she needed to shop for spring clothes, she had to practice skating, and she wanted dates with her friends. "There's a great new movie out. Everyone's going. Wanna come?" Jennifer had shaken her head. They used to be my friends, she thought.

And now even her mother had left her alone. The reporters had finally given up and disappeared. And she said she had to get back to work. She had gone to meet a client.

At the door she hesitated. "I have to earn a living, Jen," she had said. "I hate to leave you like this, but they want to see what I've come up with. I can't put it off any longer. Look, when I get back, why don't we take Cleo for a walk?"

"I can't."

"Honey, nobody's even going to look at you. Nobody cares as much as you think they do."

"I can't."

"No, Jen. What you can't do is hide here for the rest of your life."

"Well," she had screamed at her, "*do* something! Figure out a way to get rid of them!"

"I don't know how, Jen. I wish I did. You must have made them happen somehow. Somehow you must have wanted them."

"Well, I don't now!" And she had run into her room and slammed the door — again.

Her mother had followed. "Honey, you can't go on like this." She stood quietly in the doorway. "I just can't fix everything, sweetheart. I wish I could. If I knew what to do, you know I'd do anything. But I" — there was a long, helpless pause — "don't." She looked at the floor for a moment, pressed her lips together as if preparing herself for something. "Jen." She plunged in. "Jen, I think we ought to call Dr. Stevens."

"No!"

"Just to talk. Anything you tell a doctor is confidential. He won't say anything unless you tell him he can."

"No!"

"Jen." She looked at her watch anxiously. "I have to go. I'm sorry. Look, I promise I won't call him unless you say it's all right. But I think we ought to talk about it when I get back."

* * *

Now Jennifer slammed the freezer door and the refrigerator shook.

"I can't stand it," she screamed at it. How did she
know that her mother wasn't talking to the doctor
right now? She probably wasn't with a client at all.
How did she know there even was a client? A new
sob caught in her throat. There had to be a way to
get rid of them somehow! She headed for the bathroom
and opened the medicine cabinet. Maybe something
in there would help. Her eyes ran over the shelves:
cold medicine, aspirin, Tylenol, toothpaste, deodor-
ant, wart remover. It was left over from when she had
had warts on her feet. It had taken weeks to get rid
of them but all you had to do was put it on. After it
stopped sizzling you scraped at it with a razor blade
until it . . .

"Yeach!" She shuddered violently. That was gross.

She slammed the door and there was her reflection
staring back. She hated it! She grabbed a towel and
flung it over the door, then ran.

She hadn't even wanted the dumb wings! She shivered. She didn't even know how it happened. All she
had done was draw a couple of wings.

Suddenly she stiffened. A sudden stillness filled her.
She closed her eyes and stood very quietly.

In her mind she saw it all again; how she had gone
to the anatomy book, drawn the wings, been so careful
to be anatomically correct. Then she had taken the
pencils her mother had . . . The pencils — it was those
pencils. She hadn't looked at them since.

Now she went to the desk and slowly slid the drawer
open. A faint glimmer flickered in the darkness.

"The pencils," she breathed. On her nighttable the drawing was still there, propped up against her lamp. She picked it up and studied it, her head pounding. If only she could remember exactly where she had drawn those wings. There were no traces of them left on the paper. None at all.

She held up the drawing to the mirror and stared at the two images together: the real, winged Jennifer and the portrait. If the wings had somehow gotten transferred once . . . Her mother's voice came filtering through. "If you got 'em," she had said, "there must be a way to unget 'em."

That's it! The scientific principle was the same!

She sat down slowly and stared at the picture. "OK," she said out loud. She had to think this out very carefully and it helped to hear it. "What if I draw another picture of me without wings? Maybe they'll transfer back. But" — the reasoning voice within her was emphatic — "where would Dawn go? Back to the first drawing, or maybe there would end up being two of me!" She shook her head and threw that idea away. It was too complicated. She looked at the drawing again, almost squinting at it. There was no sign that the wings had ever been there. It was just a picture of her. It didn't even look as if it had been erased.

"Erased," she murmured.

Everything seemed to stop around her. "Erased."

She swept her stuff off her desk, then carefully put the drawing in the middle of the empty desk. She pulled open the drawer and looked down on the pencils.

Her heart sank. There were no erasers on the tips of the pencils. Not one.

She sat stunned, watching the opalescence deepen as the room darkened around her. Then she closed the drawer.

No, she was right; she knew she was. She could feel it.

Maybe it didn't have to be a magic eraser. But none of her regular pencils had decent erasers. They were all dirty, little pink stubs way down below the metal part. Most of them were crushed flat. There had to be one somewhere. She rummaged frantically through her top drawer. Under some wrinkled origami paper her fingers closed over something rubbery, a little rainbow eraser. It must have been a party favor sometime. She set it on the desk alongside the self-portrait, then drew in a deep breath. On her back she felt Dawn move with the stirrings of a butterfly. She poised over the drawing and a pang of loss swept through her. If she did this she would have to let them go. And it had been so wonderful! The lightness and the power and the freedom of the sky opened up around her again. She knew what it felt like to be caught by the wind and soar. She could remember. How could she let it go?

"But I want to go to the movies," a voice inside her begged. "I want to go to school. I want to skate!"

She gripped herself and bent over the drawing.

She began to erase the empty space where she thought she had drawn the original wings. She bent over it closely. She had to be careful not to touch any part of her hair or shoulders. She couldn't erase any part of herself.

Shaking, she stepped back to look at it. There was no difference on the paper, no faint image. She had thought it would gradually appear, like a Polaroid. But there was nothing. Over and over the drawing she went, all the time trying to feel a difference on her back. Was there a lightness as the wings were erased? Was there any difference at all?

Concentrating and erasing over and over until she was sure not a mark could be left, she went over it. And when she finally finished, she was sure.

In the mirror her wings peeped out from behind her.

She turned sideways. They were sort of dripping sadly down her back, still beautiful, but limp. A little less glowing, maybe.

Maybe they knew she was trying to get rid of them.

Was she trembling or were they doing that all on their own? She closed her eyes. Dismay and gratitude, happiness and hopelessness filled her all at once.

"Oh, Cleo, what am I going to do now?"

She got undressed and into bed. When her mother came in she pretended to be asleep.

Sometime during the night she turned over onto her back for the first time in more than two weeks. And in her sleep she gave a long sigh of relief.

# *21*

# *Freestyle*

"Isn't it beautiful!" Jennifer and her mother were passing the bridal shop on the way to The Rink. The dress in the window was all white lace and it seemed to dance with the reflection of the leaves that quivered in the summer breeze. Today was the freestyle test and Jennifer was skating.

"You'd look beautiful in it, sweetheart." Jennifer's mother shifted a box of homemade cookies to her other hand. "You know, it sort of looks like your skating costume."

They had bought the white skating dress. It was edged with pale blue and had long, tight sleeves. They thought it was perfect for the dove.

"Don't you want to wait here for Angela?"

"No, I told her I'd meet her upstairs. Oh, Mom, I'm so nervous!"

Her mother reached out and squeezed her hand. "You're going to be great," she said.

It had been two days after Dawn had disappeared that Jennifer had called Penelope to ask how she was, and Penelope had asked her if she'd like to go to The Rink.

"You mean you can skate?" Jennifer couldn't believe it.

"Not yet — but in a week or two I can. They won't let me jump or anything, and Reggie won't let me take the test with my cast on."

"Then how come you're practicing?"

This time Penelope sounded surprised. "I didn't hurt my legs," she said. "It's just my arm now. I can still practice edges and stuff."

"Oh."

They had met Angela there. Jennifer had eyed Don nervously as she charged out of the dressing room. "What happened to the drapes?" he had asked as the girls rushed by.

"Truck ran over 'em," she said.

"Dog ate 'em," said Angela as she pulled on her gloves. The two girls had glared at each other. Penelope had looked confused, but Don hadn't seemed to notice. "Too bad. I thought they were kinda cute," he said.

Jennifer stared at the ice. She was almost afraid to step out on it. "Do you think I'll remember how?" she had whispered to Angela as she looked out onto the smooth, white surface and tried to picture herself out there, on her own, without Dawn. But somehow her body had remembered what to do. She was surprised that it felt so easy; better than it had before. The ice felt like cold velvet as her skate glided over the surface snow and she felt her edge dig into the ice and heard the "wzz" of it as she spun. When she picked up speed to try her first jump her heart began to pound; she didn't know if she could do it without Dawn. She bent into it, sprang, and she landed it! It felt like flying! As she turned around Angela almost leaped into her arms. And Jennifer had jumped it again and again.

But it was her lessons that had been the real test.

"I can't believe it!" Scott had stared as she bent into her outside spiral. "Are you sure you're Jennifer Rosen? The one who couldn't get her leg up?" She had nodded happily. "What happened to you, monkey? It's beautiful!"

And her heart sang.

"I've been practicing, and Penelope's been helping me." She felt a little shy. "Is it really better?"

"Well, I don't know. Try it again. Just to make sure I wasn't seeing things."

It was true, she thought, as she sailed through it. She might not look like Penelope. But she didn't look like a pump handle anymore, either.

"Wow!" he said.

And she began to love it again.

"Isn't she great!" Angela had skated out for her lesson. She circled them, grinning.

Scott nodded. "Are you sure you didn't put some kind of magic in her?" The two girls stared at each other. "Like the spirit of Sonja Henie?"

"Sonja Who-ie?" Angela smirked and broke away, spinning into a series of three turns.

"Don't tell me you've been practicing, too?" Scott was incredulous. "I don't believe it! I don't know if I can stand it!"

"Oh, you know me," Angela's voice had her usual lilt. "Always working! Work, work, work, work, work!" Again she skated circles around him. "Besides, I've been helping her."

Scott struck his forehead with his hand and moaned.

"Oh, no!" He rolled his eyes. "Well, Jen, there goes your program down the tubes. We'd better put in some extra work. Let's go from dumde dum, de dum."

That had been weeks ago. Today she was going to have to do it for real, in front of people. There was even a real judge coming. Her dad had said he was going to try to make it.

"Jen!" Down the block Angela had turned the corner and was waving madly. Her parents were almost running to keep up with her.

"I can't believe I'm so nervous!" she panted as they came up. "Are you?"

Jennifer rolled her eyes and pulled open the door. "Hey, look."

Above the stair rail a huge bunch of pastel balloons floated, pulling at their strings.

"Oh, wow! Do you think that's for us?"

"Look." Angela ran her hands across the strings and the balloons bobbed frantically, tugging as if wanting to get away. "They say 'The Rink' on them. Can you believe it?"

Jennifer felt a surprising surge of new jitters. Behind them the door had opened again. "I didn't know this was going to be such a big deal!" a new voice exclaimed.

Jennifer's eyes traveled up the narrow stairwell. On the landing a crowd was blocking the door to The Rink. It was pushing through. Or trying to. A dozen people had bunched up and were jammed there. Jostling, standing on tiptoe, they strained to see over the bobbing heads in front of them. "Oh, no," — it was barely a whisper — "it's a zoo."

Jennifer reached for her mother's hand and felt another little reassuring squeeze.

"Did you know it was going to be like this?" Her mother sounded a little worried. Angela's mother shook her head, bewildered.

"I had no idea, Kate," she said. "I thought this was going to be a little exhibition or something. But this!" The sentence hung midair. "You'd think it was the Olympics."

Jennifer's heart jolted, then started a steady thudding. In front of them the mob shuffled forward a few steps, then came to a stop again. Behind them more people were trudging up the stairs, and down below the door opened again. Anxious faces peered up at them.

"How do you get in?"

Her mother looked down at them and shrugged. "I think you girls ought to take the plunge. You've got a better chance than we do. Jen, you take the cookies. I think there's going to be a table set up."

"Come on, Jen!" Angela's eyes were shining with excitement again. They gripped hands and as they poised on the edge of the crowd, they began their countdown: "One, twooo, threee . . ."

"Geronimo!" Angela bellowed.

They plowed in. "Skaters coming through, skaters coming through!" They pushed through the sea of people, and somehow a narrow path opened then closed in behind them in a wave. Every once in a while Jennifer heard a little yelp as her skates poked someone.

"Sorry," she murmured as they maneuvered through. "Sorry. Sorry." In the middle of the sea they stopped. "Which way?"

"Angela! Jen!" They heard their names over the

general din. Stacey was popping up above the heads. They waved, plunged again, and headed her way.

"How's Dawn Twitching today?" The sweet voice was all too familiar.

"What's Samantha doing here?" Jennifer rolled her eyes, then felt a little dig in the ribs from Angela.

"How come you're here, Samantha? You don't skate."

"Oh, I thought I'd come and find out how good you two are. Where's your friend Dawn Twitching today?"

"She's disappeared. Didn't you hear?" Jennifer tried to sound tragic.

"What?" For once Samantha didn't know what to say.

Jennifer nodded solemnly. "She's missing." She wished that she could make herself cry the way they did on the soaps.

"Oh." Samantha looked confused. "Look, there's David with his sister. She's really a wonderful skater. I've got to go talk to her." Samantha turned away and Jennifer watched her duck into the crowd. "Hello, David." Samantha's singsong voice rang over the chatter.

Jennifer turned away. It was odd that she used to care what Samantha said, she thought with surprise; she really didn't care anymore. Somehow, she thought, it was just dumb. "Come on, I've got to get rid of Mom's cookies before they're crumbs." They elbowed their way through the mob toward Stacey.

"Hi. Wow, look at that!"

A table was piled high with goodies. Jennifer pushed one plate of brownies over to make room for her mom's pecan maple lace cookies. There were white sugar doughnuts. And cookies. And cupcakes topped with whirls of pale frosting and paper cups brimming with pale lemonade. And in the middle of it all was a cake.

"Wow. I've never seen anything that big! Can we eat it?" Angela leaned over it. "Look, our names are on it, Jen."

"No kidding?"

Curving around the rim Jennifer's name was gracefully written in blue sugar script.

"I don't believe it! Look, there's 'Angela.' Where's yours, Stace?"

They followed the script spiraling in toward the center. In the middle was a white frosted ice skate.

"I didn't know that many kids were skating."

"Do we each get the piece with our name on it?"

"Yeah, smooth. Then Ann would hardly get anything at all."

"And Jennifer would pig out."

"Huh?" Jennifer was hardly paying attention. Around them the familiar, cozy room was packed with people she had never seen before. Penelope was weaving her way through the crowd, waving her cast at them.

"I'm sorry I'm late," she said. "Mom had me practicing left-handed piano for an hour before I could come. She's coming up." Penelope smiled her shy smile. "I told her I did some of your choreography," she said apologetically, "so she wants to see it. I can't wait for you to go on." She was squeezing Jennifer's hand. "You're going to be so good! Is your father coming?"

"I don't know." Jennifer's heart jumped, and her eyes went to the door. It was almost impossible to see everyone over the crowd.

Angela tugged on Jennifer's arm. "Come on, let's go change." Jennifer lost her grip on her skates and dropped them with a clop.

She shuffled her foot to locate them but there were

too many legs in the way. "That was dumb," she said as she leaned over to look for them. "How do you do it, Angela?"

The skates were caught between a man's feet. She looked up at him. " 'Scuse me." But he was too busy talking to hear. She pulled on his jacket, but he brushed her hand away. "Excuse me," she yelled.

His voice rose over the hubbub. "Win," he was saying. "Of course, they've been skating since they were three years old and . . ."

Jennifer crouched down to get a better look. The laces were wrapped around his ankles. How did that happen? One step and he'd go over. He'd hit like a rock. She could just hear Angela yelling, "Timber!" She reached up and pulled on his jacket. "Of course," he boomed, "I used to play hockey in high school. Nothing like this of course, but I was pretty good."

"Oh, for pete's sake." She reached between his feet and fumbled with the knot.

"Hey, what the hell's going on down there?" She looked up.

"Dropped my skates," she answered loudly. "They're all tangled."

"Well, why didn't you say so," he boomed, "instead of fooling around with my feet?" He picked up his foot and she scrambled to unwind the laces. She yanked at one skate; nothing happened. Now it was caught under someone's high heel. She tried to pull at it, but nothing happened. Maybe if I tickled her ankle.

"Can I help?" David's curious face gazed down at her.

Ohmagod! Why did he always have to see her doing something strange? Nothing ever changed, wings or not.

"It's caught," she panted. "I can't get it."

"Oh, Mom, will you lift your foot? Her skate's caught."

Oh, help, she almost tickled his mother's foot. She clasped the skates to her chest and struggled up. "Thanks," she murmured.

"I guess you're skating," he said. "So's my sister."

"She is?"

"Yeah, she's going for Freestyle Three."

"Wow! She must be good."

"I guess so. She's fifteen. She's been skating for a million years, so she oughta be."

"I'm just going for One."

"Well, I guess you're pretty good."

Jennifer shuffled her feet. "I don't know."

She felt a tap on her shoulder. "Better get ready, Rosen." Don was ambling through the crowd on his way to the back room. "You're not even changed yet and we're going to start in a few minutes."

"Jen, come on." Angela grabbed her.

Fear tightened in her chest again. They ducked into the tiny locker room to change.

When they emerged the atmosphere was changed. The chatter and small talk was gone; the gaiety had disappeared, disintegrated into a gripping tension that had a firm hold on the whole room. The first group of skaters pressed up against the windows, staring out at the rink, and behind them everyone else jostled for position. People were pressed into each other, some standing on benches to get a better view. Faces were set and anxious. The skaters paced, clasping and unclasping their hands, putting on and taking off their gloves. Some huddled together in tight little groups; friends squeezed each other's hands as they stood together, silent and tense. Jennifer felt breathless.

Reggie and the judge were already on the ice. They were bundled up in ski jackets and ear muffs and scarves, hunched over a table set up on the side. They shuffled papers with mittened hands. Scott stood at the top of the stairs to the rink.

And in the center of the ice a tiny girl had taken her position.

Behind her Jennifer heard a woman coo, "Isn't she sweet?"

"So adorable."

Jennifer didn't think she looked adorable. She thought she looked scared. Her face was pale, her costume was all black. Her skinny legs looked even skinnier with the big white boots sticking out at the bottom. Jennifer thought she looked like a tiny, skating Greek widow in mourning that she had seen in the *National Geographic* magazines at the doctor's office.

"Go get 'em, kid!" A man's voice rang out over the low, tense murmur of the crowd. "Show 'em what a six-year-old can do!" The tiny girl swayed a little as she stared straight ahead.

Jennifer touched Penelope's hand. "I'd hate to go first," she whispered and felt Penelope nodding beside her. She stood up on her toe picks looking for her mother. She smiled and waved. And then she clutched at Angela's arm. "Look," she gasped, "my dad's here!"

Across the room and over the heads, her father lifted his fingers in the V for Victory sign. "Ohmagod, my dad's here!" she said and bit her lip. Her heart lurched again. Behind her David was standing on a bench to see the rink better. Samantha was standing next to him, giggling. Jennifer's mother was holding on to Angela's mother, a bewildered look on her face. She smiled, and nodded encouragingly. But she was pale

and her face had a strained look to it. Jennifer tried
to smile back as she felt in her sleeve for the tiny,
folded bit of pink chiffon she had put there for luck.
It was still there, tucked in tightly against her wrist.
Angela clutched her hand and Jennifer clutched it
back.

"Quiet, please!" At the top of the steps Scott put
up a hand. The hum turned into sudden silence. "Our
first little skater is Valerie Cruise. She will be skating to
a selection from Franz Liszt's Hungarian Rhapsodies."

"Go get 'em, kid!" shouted the father.

The music started.

One by one they skated.

By the time they had gotten to Angela they had
heard "Over the Rainbow" three times and "Put On
a Happy Face" twice. A few skaters looked wonderful.
Two kids had fallen and Jennifer had gasped with
everyone else. She had seen the first girl get up, her
face tight with fear, tears forming behind her eyes. But
she had started again and had managed to get through
her routine without falling again. The applause had
been very loud for her when she finished. She came
off the ice and ran sobbing into her mother's arms.

Some kids had been asked to repeat the steps and
they had gone to the center of the ice shakily and
done it. Legs had gone up in spirals, straight or crooked,
and jumps had been landed one way or another. As
each skater came off the ice applause burst from the
crowd. Their friends screamed and cheered. Reggie
and the judge bent over their papers, recorded the
skater's marks, then handed them out to Scott. All
eyes followed those bits of paper as they were handed

head over head to Don in the back room. No one would even know until the end if she passed.

"Our next little skater is Angela MacDonald." Scott's voice brought them back to the rink.

Jennifer's heart leaped up again. It was thumping so wildly that she was hardly aware of anything else. Angela pulled her sweatshirt up over her head and grinned. Jennifer bit her lip and Angela headed toward the ice.

Everyone else had started their routines in the middle of the ice, posing, like the first girl in black. The music started, but Angela wasn't on yet. Heads turned, looking for the skater.

"And our next little skater is Angela MacDonald," Scott announced again.

"Maybe she's too scared," a voice whispered.

The music kept going: "If there's a wrong way to do it, nobody does it like meeeee."

Suddenly a ragged figure burst onto the ice. She raced up to the judge and did a hockey stop. The ice sprayed out at him and she stared in mock horror. Then she threw up her hands and backed off, hiding her face in her hands. Jennifer, Penelope, and Angela had gone over and over this part. It had to be just right.

It took a moment for the crowd to catch on but when she turned around, raised her eyes to the heavens, and folded her hands in prayer, her lips moving inaudibly, someone began to chuckle and then the whole room broke up.

She was just as loose and sloppy as always. And when she ended her routine, sprawled out over the ice, her mouth opened wide in a surprised "OH!" they broke out into real cheers. When she stumbled across the ice to the door on her ankles and almost fell down the stairs they were hysterical.

Giggling, she grinned up at Scott and he reached out, laughing, and ruffled her hair. In a second she was surrounded.

It took some time before it was calm again and she could manage to make her way back to Penelope and Jennifer. "It was so great!" Jennifer was hugging her.

"They couldn't believe it!" Penelope was almost jumping up and down.

"I think the judge is still in shock." Angela giggled again. "Did you see his face when I zipped up on him?"

"Quiet, please. Our next skater is Christopher . . ."

They turned. Everything was tense again.

Halfway through the test a tiny little girl in red shot out onto the ice. Nobody had ever seen her before. Hair flying, feet dancing, she flew through her routine like quicksilver. "Wow, who is she? She even looks like she's having fun," whispered Penelope.

"You're next," whispered Angela.

"Ohmagod," gasped Jennifer.

She swallowed hard. The quicksilver girl was finished.

"Skater coming through. Skater coming through," Angela chanted cheerfully as she led Jennifer through the cheers. Jennifer was suddenly numb. She couldn't remember her steps. How did her program start? What was her music? She didn't want to look at anyone. She felt for her little piece of chiffon. It was still there.

"Just don't try the Jennifer Jump," whispered Angela as her friend started up the steps.

Then somehow Jennifer was posing. All the faces

were out there waiting: her mother, her father, Penelope, Samantha. All those eyes, she thought.

"It's just another practice session," she murmured to herself as the thumping in her chest got wilder. She tried to take those slow even breaths her mother was always talking about. Where was the music? Just another practice. The white ice surrounded her.

Then her music started and she remembered.

# 22

# Happiness

"Jen!" Angela was racing down the street after her.

They had all had hot chocolate at the French bakery to celebrate; the kind with mounds of whipped cream over the top and melting, like a swirling cirrus cloud, into the steaming cocoa.

They were all so tired and stuffed. After the cake and brownies and lemonade upstairs, Penelope's mother had insisted on taking them all out. It was the end of a magical evening, to be sitting in the elegant little bakery looking out.

"I'm so proud of you," her father said.

"I really thought you'd get it," Angela complained. Someone else had won first prize for Freestyle One, the quicksilver girl in the red skating dress. But Jennifer didn't care. She had her own medal for Most Improvement. She couldn't stop looking at it or feeling it in her hand. And her dad had come all the way from Florida to see her skate. And David had asked if she'd like to go biking on Saturday. Everything was fine.

Little by little the excitement ebbed and now the group leaned back in their chairs in a kind of happy stupor. "Well," Jennifer's mother was the first to finally stir, "shall we try to waddle on home, sweetheart?" They had all groaned as they pushed back their chairs and stood up. Now they were going their separate ways. Penelope and her mother grabbed a cab and were off and even Jennifer's father had to leave. But she'd see him tomorrow; he'd be able to stay for a few days.

"You were great," her mother said as they started for home. She reached for her daughter's hand and slipped something into it. Jennifer looked down. It was a tiny, gold ice-skate charm. "Oh, Mom, it's beautiful."

"You were wonderful, Jen. You really were."

"JEN!"

Jennifer and her mother stopped in front of the bridal shop and turned. Angela's skates were jiggling on her shoulders as she ran up the hill. The tote bag was bumping her knees.

"Wait!" She was breathless and panting as she reached them. "Jen, I know I promised not to, but I couldn't help it." She was shuffling at the bottom of her bag. "And there's no way anybody could tell."

Jennifer and her mother looked at each other as Angela delved deeper. "Here it is!" She was triumphant. She thrust a photograph into Jennifer's hand, then turned and flew back to her parents. "Call you tomorrow!"

They looked down on it, squinting under the glare of the street lamp. It was of treetops, barely budding, and a blue sky. And a string of a kite that climbed until it almost disappeared.

They stared at it, trying to make it out. Off in the distance, at the very tip of the string, high in the sky, was a tiny bump.

Jennifer turned the picture over. On the back of it Angela had scrawled, "Dawn, over Central Park."

"Leave it to Angela." Her mother shook her head and chuckled.

Jennifer reached for her mother's hand.

They were halfway home before Jennifer's mother suddenly stopped and stared. "Ohmagod," she said, "that was you!"